Max,
Your mom says you should
read more. I agree.

END OF THE LOOP

Enjoy,

End of the Loop

Brent Nichols

Cover Art and Design by
Aaron Bilawchuk

TINY SLEDGEHAMMER
CANADA

End of the Loop

Brent Nichols — First Edition

Copyright © 2020 Brent Nichols

Tiny Sledgehammer

An Imprint of The Seventh Terrace

41 Mt. Yamnuska Place SE

Calgary, Alberta, Canada, T2Z 2Z6

www.the-seventh-terrace.com

Publisher's Note: This is a work of fiction. Names, characters, places, and incidents are a product of the author's imagination. Locales and public names are sometimes used for atmospheric purposes. Any resemblance to actual people, living or dead, or to businesses, companies, events, institutions, or locales is completely coincidental.

Cover Art and Design by Aaron Bilawchuk

ISBN 978-1-9992001-7-6

For Tammy, who is full of awesomeness.

One

It was a spring morning when they changed David's medication and he started to remember.

The nurse's office had a window, and he saw pale green shoots of grass in the withered lawn outside. He was pretty sure new grass meant spring.

Mornings were the clearest time for David. The orderly would prod him out of bed, lead him through the corridors, and bring him to the office for his orange pill. Soon after that the world went fuzzy and warm, the details lost in a soft haze.

Sometimes he had another clear period in the evening, usually stealing over him in the TV room. He would stare at the screen, trying to make sense of whatever show was on, until an orderly tapped his shoulder and led him once again to the office.

But he took two pills in the evening, not one, and it washed the memories away. So, when he looked back, he saw a chain of early mornings. Only the grass outside ever changed.

Waking up was an incremental process that was by no means complete by the time the orderly was done pushing David's limbs into his clothes. Even the walk from his room to the security station was like something on TV, happening to someone else. Lift a foot, put it down, repeat until the hand on your shoulder tightens and pulls you to a stop.

The growl of a buzzer made him flinch. Metal clicked, and habit put his feet into motion before the orderly could nudge him forward. Half a step sideways, through a doorway, pause until you hear the heavy steel door clang shut. One more click, and the gentle pressure of a hand on his arm.

The lights were brighter on this side of the security station. He smelled flowers and dust and a hint of cologne. Cool air touched the tops of his ears as he walked under a ceiling vent.

They passed a bulletin board, just a blur of bright rectangles in his peripheral vision. A painting showed a man and a woman dancing, her dress a dramatic sweep of red fabric. By the time he realized he wanted to turn his head for a better look, he was already several steps away.

They stopped, as always, in the doorway to the office. David squinted at the sunlight flooding in through the window on the back wall. The nurse was no more than a silhouette. "Come in. Have a seat."

The orderly guided him forward, then pressed down on David's shoulders. He sat on a small wooden chair. The nurse perched on the corner of a wide desk, making a notation on a tablet that rested on her leg. "How are you feeling, David? How did you sleep?"

He stared at her leg, which was covered in peach scrubs. *That's not right. It's supposed to be green.* He tilted his gaze up. The nurse, a petite Asian woman with enormous glasses, made a note on her tablet, not waiting for him to reply.

It's a different nurse. He rubbed the side of his head, trying to remember what the usual nurse looked like.

A fat red mug sat on the desk beside her leg, and he caught a faint whiff of coffee. It tickled at the roots of his memory, tantalizing him with the idea that the past was there, just out of reach. The cup, he decided, was familiar. Sometimes it sat on the black surface of the desk. Sometimes it perched on stack of papers.

"Here you go," she said, and held out a small paper cup. Her voice was familiar. *It's the same nurse,* he decided. *I never looked at her face before.* For some reason the thought disturbed him, sending anxious prickles across his shoulders.

"David?" She waggled the little cup, and he took it, dumping it onto his palm. He was back on familiar ground now. The round orange pill would sweep away his discomfort. The prickles would vanish until the cycle repeated tomorrow. He gave the cup back to the nurse and took a cup of water in exchange. He lifted his hand toward his mouth, then froze.

There were two pills in his palm. One was round and red. The other was triangular, and pink.

"It's all right, David."

He stared at the pills.

She said, "It's not good to take chlorpromazine for too long. You get dystonia." She tapped the skin below her ear. "Remember how your neck was sore? Anyway, a change in medication should clear it right up." She made an encouraging gesture. "Go ahead. Pop it in."

A phone rang, the sound startling him. He lowered his hand as the nurse twisted around and reached across the desk. She spoke into the phone as he stared first at the pills and then at the water. He lifted the cup to his lips and took a sip.

The nurse glanced at him, gave him an approving smile, and stood. She hung up the phone, then came toward him with a tongue depressor in her hand. David opened his mouth automatically, enduring the dry touch of the strip of wood. It was just like every morning, except for the pills growing sticky in his fist.

"Now, you might have withdrawal symptoms. Nausea. Shakiness." She peered at him. "You don't understand me, do you?" She put a hand on her stomach. "Your tummy might be upset. You have to tell us if you don't feel good. Okay?" She waited, and when he didn't respond she looked past his shoulder and nodded.

Fingers touched David's arm and tugged upward, urging him to his feet. The orderly steered him out of the office and down the corridor.

But I didn't take my pill. David stopped, only to have the orderly tug impatiently on his arm. He walked, mute, sure he should do something but unable to figure out what.

They passed through another security station, and another steel door clanged shut behind them. David didn't notice when the hand on his arm let go, but the orderly was gone when a woman in a hairnet handed him a plastic tray.

Taking the tray without opening his fist was awkward, but he managed it. A woman in shapeless blue clothes moved along a steel counter, sliding a tray just like David's. He copied her. Across the counter a skinny man in an apron smiled as he set a bowl of cereal on David's tray. "Hey, buddy, how are you this morning?"

David stopped, sure there was an appropriate response. It was there, on the tip of his tongue .... But the man had already turned away, and a fierce-looking woman appeared at David's elbow, fingers gripping a tray. She crowded against him, and he retreated, moving along the counter.

The next moment of clarity came as he sat down at a long, scratched metal table. His tray now held a napkin, a spoon, a glass of water, and a plate with a slice of dry toast. He couldn't have said where any of it came from.

When he finally opened his fist, the pills stuck to his palm. He used his napkin to pick them free, then balled up the square of paper and dropped it on his tray.

Habit took over. A corner of his mind watched as he ate. He couldn't remember previous breakfasts, but a comforting sense of familiarity told him this was what he usually did. That, and the mechanical way his body moved, spooning up every bite of cereal before lifting the bowl to his lips to drink the milk, then reaching for the toast. *I wonder what I'll do next.*

When the food was gone he stood. *Where am I going?* The thought was enough to break the tenuous thread of habit, and he froze. A man across the table rose and picked up a tray, and David copied him. Habit once again urged him into motion, but he planted his feet and resisted. He looked around, then closed his eyes.

He couldn't remember a single detail about the room.

He opened his eyes and looked again. This time he forced himself to focus. It was maddeningly difficult, like trying to grab a handful of air, but he gritted his teeth and made himself give a name to the first thing he saw.

Table. That's a table. It's right in front of me. I was just sitting there.

He inhaled, exhaled, and blinked his eyes. *Table.* The concept remained, not fading into the mist that still pressed close on every side.

He kept looking, turning his head from left to right. It was a long table, a rectangle of scuffed, scratched metal decorated with red plastic trays. Half a dozen chairs lined either side, most of them occupied. Men and women in baggy blue clothes ate cereal or nibbled on toast. A heavyset man rocked from side to side and muttered to himself. The others ignored him.

David recognized none of them, and he shivered, not sure why the thought bothered him. *Do I eat breakfast with them every day? Who are they?*

He turned away, seeking distraction, and found himself looking at another table just like his own. Half the chairs were empty, and as he watched, a pair of men rose. They carried their trays to a rack against one wall, chatting as they walked. One man laughed, and the other joined in as they slid their trays into slots in the rack.

David carried his own tray across the room, thinking about their laughter, feeling a strange hollow sensation under his breastbone. He didn't want anyone to talk to him. He had no idea how to respond. But he felt ... alone.

Aside from the two tables, the only significant feature in the room was the counter that ran from wall to wall, separating the kitchen staff from the dining area. David racked his tray, then looked at the counter, furrowing his brow. Something about the layout of the room troubled him, a thought he couldn't quite pin down.

"Hey." Something bumped David's arm. He turned, and a short, scowling woman prodded him with the edge of her breakfast tray. "You're blocking the road."

He stared at her, mystified, and she poked him once more with the tray. Then she pressed the tray against his arm and kept on pressing, eyebrows drawn together and down until he wondered how she could see. He backed away from her, heard a clatter as his shoulders hit the tray rack, and edged sideways.

She pushed past him, slid her tray into the rack, shot him a last furious glance, and bustled away.

He stared after her, then cringed as several more people advanced on him, trays in their hands. He scurried aside.

One by one, people finished their meals, then drifted to one corner, gathering in a loose cluster near a set of double doors. David sidled over and stood on the fringe of the group. After a time a buzzer sounded and the doors swung open. He shuffled along with the others, flinching when the doors clicked shut behind him.

This new room was about twice the size of the dining area, and much more comfortable. There were sofas and padded chairs, tables of various sizes, and a large TV on one wall. David walked to a couch near the TV. *I remember this.* He rubbed his forehead, trying to tease out the impression that danced through the mist. *From the evenings. This is the TV room.*

He stared at a dimpled impression in one end of a long couch. *Here. I always sit here.* He sat, nodding to himself. This felt right. This was the seat from which he would be roused and led back to the office for his evening pills. The chain of evening visits was a dim memory stretching back into mist. *But what about the rest of the day?* He realised he didn't know what else he did.

On the TV screen a woman sat behind a desk, smiling and speaking, her words little more than gibberish. A man and another woman nodded, made interjections, and laughed at her jokes.

The next show featured two men, faces serious as they spoke to one another.

The commercials were his favourite part. They vibrated with drama and ended before his mind could wander. None of it made much sense, but it mesmerized him.

He didn't look away until the screen went dark. The couches and chairs around him were all full. Some people got to their feet. Others stared at the blank TV.

"I hope they have jello today. Do you think there's jello?"

"There's always jello. I'm sick of jello. Why can't we get some ...."

The voices trailed off as the speakers moved away. David stood and looked around. People in blue shuffled toward the doors leading back to the dining area. He looked down at himself. He wore the same blue clothes as the others. *Pyjamas.* He plucked at his shirt, thinking about the word surfacing in his mind. *I'm wearing pyjamas.*

It's the middle of the day and I'm wearing pyjamas. His fingers twisted at the fabric. Why did it suddenly feel so odd, so embarrassing, to be dressed in blue pyjamas?

"Come on. Lunch time. Let's go. You don't want to miss lunch, do you? There's jello." The voice belonged to an orderly, a large man in dark blue scrubs. A man and a woman still sat staring at the TV. The orderly went to each of them. Stepping into the man's field of vision was enough to get the man up and moving. The woman didn't react until the orderly tapped her shoulder, then tugged on her elbow, urging her to her feet.

Patient. Another new word rose in David's mind, and he examined it. *We're patients here.* At first glance the orderlies and patients looked the same, dressed in similar plain clothing. The scrubs were subtly different, though, aside from colour. Or perhaps it was body language that made it unmistakable that the orderlies were in charge, and the patients were under their control.

The doors to the dining room swung open and David moved along with the crowd. He queued up with the others, taking a red tray and lining up at the counter.

The orderlies didn't eat. A couple of them stood chatting near the doors. Another stood by the back wall. They were all men, he noticed. And they were all large. The pair near the door seemed engaged in their conversation, but they glanced frequently at the patients.

David reached the counter and a tired-looking woman passed him a plate with a sandwich on it. The plate slipped in his grasp, thumped on the tray, and came to rest, still intact. He gave the woman an anxious glance, wondering if she'd be angry, but she was already passing a plate to the next person in line.

Good thing the plate didn't fall on the floor, or she'd have to .... He played with the thought as he pushed his tray along the counter. What would she do? She couldn't pick up the plate. The counter ran from wall to wall. There was no way for the kitchen staff to reach the dining room.

No, said a cold voice in his head as he carried his tray to a table. *It's the other way around. There's no way for the patients to reach the kitchen.*

He sat, giving an uneasy glance to the orderlies by the door. *They're not here to help everyone find the dining room,* said the voice in his head. *They're here to protect the staff from the patients. From you. They're here because you're dangerous.*

He flinched away from the thought, retreating into the comforting routine of eating. He embraced the fog instead of fighting it, and he didn't look up until a woman screamed.

The scream made him jump, and he blinked, disoriented. He was back on the couch. A woman's face filled the TV screen. The terror on her face turned to indignation, and she scolded a little boy while he pulled off a rubber mask and grinned at her.

How long have I been sitting here? He shifted, feeling tight muscles in his back and legs. *Quite a while, I guess.*

The sound of laughter drew his attention back to the TV, and he forgot everything else. One show followed another, until the orderlies herded them back into the cafeteria.

There was some sort of drama on the TV after supper. A man and a woman ran through tall grass, kissed. Then they argued, and a cold hand clutched David's stomach. The woman fled in tears. The man walked away alone.

Cars moved across the screen, and something stirred in David's mind. An image, tenuous as a remembered story. A steering wheel in his hands. He had driven a car?

What changed?

An orderly tapped his shoulder. David stood. It was only when they moved through the security station that he realized he was being taken for his evening pills. His feet slowed, and the orderly gave him an absent-minded tug.

Wait a minute! Is that all there is? I watch TV and eat? While the seasons go by?

He walked obediently beside the orderly to the nurse's office where a thin young man with wispy blond hair handed David a pill cup.

David looked at the pills in the palm of his hand. There was one red pill and two pink ones. He thought of the comfortable haze they would bring. *Finally. Things will go back to normal.*

"Come on, David, let's go." The man was impatient, distracted.

David put the pills in his mouth. The red pill tasted right, but the pink pills were bitter and chalky. He gulped water. The pills swirled around, and he tried to swallow them, but his throat rebelled.

The man moved around the desk, tongue depressor in hand. If he had said, "David, did you swallow the pills?" then David would have said, "No."

But all the man said was, "Open your mouth." He glanced inside, then turned away, reaching for a tablet. "That's it." He nodded past David's shoulder. "Thanks, George."

David stared at him. The pills lay on either side of his tongue, the bitter taste puckering his mouth. He thought about spitting them out. He thought about asking for more water. But the orderly tugged on his arm, so David turned and left the office.

He stepped into his bedroom and the door clicked shut behind him. After a moment another metallic rattle came, and David turned, putting a hand on the doorknob.

They locked me in. He spat the pills into his hand, suddenly afraid. *Do they know?*

No, you fool. They lock you in every night. You just never noticed before.

The room was small and colourless, a narrow bed filling most of the floor. A doorway in the back wall opened onto a little bathroom. He stood in front of the sink, looking at the pills in his palm. They had lost all shape, merging into a single rust-coloured pellet.

Beside the sink was a small glass, and a fluted cup that held his toothbrush. He looked at the glass and thought about washing the pills down with water. Then, guided by some deeper impulse, he dropped the gooey pills into his toothbrush holder.

He washed his hand, then rinsed his mouth. Vague memories came to him as he looked around the bathroom. The orderly led him in here each morning after shaking him awake. He would be pushed half-asleep into the shower. He would half participate in his own towelling. He would brush his own teeth, when he was told to.

Apparently I don't comb my hair. David looked into the mirror over the sink, focusing on his hair, which stood up in tufts. He kept his gaze away from the thin, vacant-eyed face beneath.

There was grey in his hair, which didn't seem right. *I'm, what? Twenty? Twenty-five? Less than that, I think. Or I was when they locked me up. But how long have I been here? Christ, I could be fifty.*

Meeting his own eyes in the mirror was difficult, but he managed it. He had no crow's feet, no wrinkles, but he looked ... mature. Not young.

That isn't me. The face is wrong.

He squeezed his eyes shut, his stomach tightening. *Well, what am I supposed to look like?*

I don't know.

Then how can it be wrong?

He put a hand on his stomach, rubbing it, telling himself to unclench his abdominal muscles. His fingertips traced a ridge through the fabric of his shirt. He lifted the hem and looked at his belly.

A jagged pink line stretched from the bottom of his ribcage to his navel. He poked it uneasily. *Is that a scar? What the hell happened to me? How could I forget something like that?*

Two steps took him back into the bedroom, where he looked resentfully at the locked door. He wanted to rattle the knob, bang on the door, demand to be let out.

But then they'll know something has changed.

Why that scared him he didn't know, but he turned away without touching the door.

He shut off the light and went to bed.

Two

Wind was the first thing he felt. It rushed against his face, set his hair dancing, and pressed his clothes against his skin. The hardest gusts rocked him, making him giddy. Bright, hot sunlight turned the world rosy through his closed eyelids. He stood somewhere very high up. He knew that if he opened his eyes the view would be spectacular, but he kept them shut, savouring the moment.

Then he was indoors, with someone's warm fingertips taking slow, delicious steps from rib to rib, creeping up his chest toward his left nipple. He squirmed, trying to control it, afraid she would stop.

Warm sheets changed to cool grass against his back. Birds chirped and sang, and leaves rustled. He shifted, and the grass tickled. He laughed, and a feminine giggle joined in. They laughed together, and he stretched out a hand, knowing she would take it. The dream faded before their fingers met.

The walk up the corridor seemed longer than usual. He wanted to shrug off the orderly's hand, which never quite left his upper arm. He wanted to stop, to look around at these corridors he'd passed through so many times but never really seen.

He kept walking.

At last he sank onto the familiar chair in the nurse's office. He couldn't remember what the nurse from yesterday morning looked like, but he recognized the red coffee cup.

A plant sat on the desk behind the cup, with wiry stems a foot high and dozens of curling green leaves. David wondered idly if it was new.

Then he saw the old leaves, brown and shrivelled, scattered around the soil and on the desktop. The plant must have been there for weeks. He just hadn't seen it.

The thought bothered him. His fingers trembled as he turned to the nurse, and he was sure his distress must have showed on his face.

But the cold voice was there again in the back of his mind. *No, David. Remember your reflection last night? Remember what you look like? All she sees in your face is a blank.*

That thought disturbed him more. He didn't meet her gaze as she handed him a little paper cup.

"How's your tummy?" She patted her own stomach. "Any nausea? Stomach upset?"

He shook his head, and her eyebrows rose. *She didn't expect me to answer.*

"Well, good." She smiled. "We'll reduce your dose even further tomorrow. Pretty soon you'll just have to take the haloperidol."

He plopped the pills onto his tongue, washed them down with water, and swallowed.

He was spooning his usual breakfast cereal when the warm, fuzzy blanket settled around his mind. He sighed. *Finally. It's over.* But a final thought intruded. A memory of laughing.

David twitched. *Wait a minute. I don't want to ....* The drug's stupor took hold, and the thought slipped away.

David belched, and the movement jolted his eyes from the TV screen. His eyes swam back to their target, and he managed to follow a bit of the plot. A car chased another car. A truck pulled into the street and the first car got away.

Now a man entered a house. A woman, tall, striking, beautiful, ran into his arms. They kissed. His hands roamed her back, her mouth explored his.

Muscles clenched in David's thighs and arms. He shook his head, trying to clear the fog. This was like part of his dream! This seemed important, although he couldn't remember why.

The screen went dark. David stared at it, waiting for the lovers to reappear, until an orderly tapped him on the shoulder.

They shuffled to the office. He couldn't tell if the nurse was someone familiar or someone new.

He dropped the pills into his palm. He was getting used to how they looked and tasted. But if he swallowed these pills, he wouldn't dream tonight.

He put the pills into his mouth and looked right at the nurse while he used his tongue to shove the pills between his top lip and his gums. He drank the water.

"Open wide." The nurse pushed a depressor against his tongue and nodded. The orderly led him out.

David added the pills to his toothbrush holder and went to bed.

He was cold in the first dream. Goosebumps covered his skin. He held someone's hands, but the delicate fingers didn't respond to his touch. They were limp and cold, and slick with moisture. He looked down. His hands were covered in blood. So were hers. He could smell it, thick and cloying, with an undertone of sweat and musky perfume. He squeezed his eyes shut, but he could still see the blood. *Wake up. I need to wake up!*

The dream faded, changed. He lay on his back in a bedroom, much nicer than his little cell. Golden sunlight poured in through pale curtains. He wanted to look out the window, but the touch of fingers on his stomach distracted him. The fingers crept downward, teasing him, arousing him. He squirmed and turned.

A woman lay stretched out beside him on the bed. She was slender and beautiful, with blonde hair and chiselled features. She smiled, giggling, her eyes warm with love. She was achingly familiar.

David reached for her. She wore a filmy bra and panties, and his breath quickened as his fingers brushed her skin. He was careful, gentle, tender, but she dug urgent fingers into his shoulders, her expression greedy and impatient.

A sob shook him when the dream ended. She vanished, and the bedroom faded into black nothing, but then the sob was a gasp for breath and he was running. Grass surrounded him, the turf soft and springy under his shoes. To his left a blur of green vegetation, to his right—

He stumbled, his legs buckling, grass hitting his knees. He cried out, a wordless sound of joy and wonder at the view before him. The ground ended just a few feet away. Beyond was a valley, an immense, dizzying gulf with a river winding far below. Sunlight glittered on the waves, and birds swept along, just above the water. Distant mountains lined the horizon, jagged peaks glittering with snow.

A shrill cry drew his gaze upward. A hawk circled high above the valley, wings rigid, riding a thermal. Vast heaps of cloud made a dazzling backdrop, giving way to a sky so intensely blue it snatched the breath from his throat.

David sat upright and wailed as the panorama disappeared and his four cold walls returned.

He did not sleep again that night. Instead he lay on the bed, his muscles rigid and still while his mind raced. *Once I drove cars. Once I held a woman in my arms. What else have I done? What else have I lost?*

With the passing of hours his mind slowed, and the tumbling thoughts became clearer. *I can't lose any more. I have to get out of here.*

And it would have to be soon. His luck could not last. Soon, very soon, he would have to take his medication again, and this night would be lost in the fog that had claimed the rest of his life. He would never dream again.

A vision swam out of his memory. He lay on a metal cot, restrained by canvas straps. He screamed, thrashed, and whipped his head from side to side as vague forms in white moved around him. A needle plunged into his shoulder. Lethargy washed over him, and he stopped fighting. Drool tickled his cheek, but he lacked the strength to close his mouth.

It will happen again. Restraints. Drugs. They will never let you leave. Deep in the pit of his stomach chilly fingers plucked at him. He told himself he was worried about getting caught. The cold voice was back, though, an insidious whisper he tried to ignore. *You screamed when the needle went in. You tried to fight it. But it was a relief.*

That night, for the first time, he thought analytically about the place he was in. He thought about the locked doors, the security stations, the orderlies. There would be no easy way to escape. But he had a glimmer of an idea.

When the light came on, he was tired enough to have no trouble pretending to be in his usual pharmaceutical fog. The orderly smiled when he revived enough in the shower to dry and dress himself.

The man finally stepped out of the room when David reached for his toothbrush. A moment later he had the toothbrush jar upended. He had no idea when the jar might be cleaned. It was best to act now.

The pills, deposited damp, had congealed into one smeared lump. David wrapped it in a bit of toilet paper. His pyjamas had no pockets, so he shoved the little bundle into his underwear.

Then he brushed his teeth and straightened his wet hair as best he could with his fingers. It wouldn't dry into random spikes today.

He joined the orderly, remembering to shamble brokenly as they moved down the hall. The familiar walls seemed dreary and ugly, and he wondered what was on the other side. *Please, let me find out.*

The big hand on his arm was oppressive, an indignity. He wanted to shove the hand away, push the man back, to lash out, to ... to ....

He shuddered. He'd forgotten what anger felt like. Yet, somewhere, he remembered. Before all the drugs, he had been very angry indeed.

The orderly, he belatedly noticed, was staring at him. David lowered his head and shuffled forward. *Nothing to see here. Just another sedated patient.*

The nurse smiled automatically as they came in, reaching for her tablet as David sat down. It was someone new, and his stomach did a flip-flop. His plan wouldn't work, which was simultaneously a disappointment and a relief.

She reached behind her, produced a fat red mug, and took a sip. She set the mug down and handed him a little paper cup with his pills.

Does that mean it's the same nurse? Does it matter? He took a deep breath as he accepted the little cup. *I guess I have to do this.*

David kept his face expressionless as he put the pills in his mouth, held them against his teeth with his tongue, and swallowed the water. He pushed the pills into the empty water cup with his tongue and lowered his hand. He palmed the pills while the nurse searched his mouth.

So far, so good. But now I have to have a conversation. His plan wouldn't work with the orderly standing behind him, and his only weapon was time.

The nurse perched on the edge of the desk, her hip nudging a stack of paper, making it shift but not quite topple. "How's your tummy? Any nausea?"

"No. I mean, yes."

She raised her eyebrows.

"I have ... I had some strange dreams."

That caught her attention. She set the tablet aside and grabbed a pad of yellow paper. "Tell me about your dreams, David."

So he did. Slowly, halting, because he wasn't used to conversation, and because he was supposed to be drugged, and because he had to kill time.

He stammered and repeated himself, adding a new detail each time the nurse started to lower the notepad. And finally the orderly shifted behind him.

"It's all right, George. Go ahead. I'll call you when he's ready to go."

The door behind David opened and closed, and his heart beat faster.

"Go on, David. What next?"

She smiled encouragingly, then looked down, flipping a page in the notepad. David mumbled something while he plunged one hand into his underwear. By the time she looked back he had the paper-wrapped bundle in his hand, below the level of her desktop.

She took a sip and the smell of coffee washed over David, tantalizing him with ghostly images of his lost life and steeling his resolve.

He fumbled the toilet paper aside, dropped it, and held the lump of medication in his hand. He put the morning's pills with the others. It was now or never.

"Um, then there was this huge valley. And the sky. And it was this wide!"

He flung his arms out to demonstrate, his left wrist scything across the desktop, inches above the scarred wood. Her pencil jar spilled, and the plant with the curling green leaves toppled to the floor, dirt cascading across the carpet. The nurse popped to her feet, edging around the desk to pick up the plant.

And David opened his right hand and dropped his collection of pills into her coffee.

Three

In a moment the worst of the damage was corrected, dirt scooped into the pot and pencils collected. David sat back in his chair, trying to look abashed.

The woman gave him one searching, speculative glance. He blushed, and she smiled. "It's okay, David. These things happen."

She sat once again on the edge of the desk. She took a sip of coffee, then made an extensive note on the yellow pad. The silence stretched out as David stared at the mug.

She put the pad down, smiling. "Okay. So, there was a beach. Pretty exciting. Then what?"

She picked up her cup, took a sip.

He started describing the river valley. When he ran out of specific memories he made things up, inventing encounters with cast members from yesterday's TV shows. The nurse watched him intently, scribbling fast notes while he talked.

He realized he was speaking too quickly, too clearly, and showing too much emotion. She would change his medication after this. But he had all her attention as the level of her coffee cup dropped lower and lower.

Finally she put the cup down empty, and he stopped. His throat felt tired and dry. *I would kill for a sip of that coffee. No! Not kill ....*

"Was there anything else in the dream, David?"

"No."

She stared at him, not quite focussing on his eyes. Then her gaze slid upward until she was staring into the air a foot above his head. She shook herself and looked back at him.

"Um, let's see. Any, uh, any physical symptoms? How do you feel?"

"I feel okay."

"My, aren't you the talkative one today. Let's check your blood pressure."

She stood, wobbled for a moment, then leaned over and grabbed the desk. She kept a hand on the desk as she circled around and dropped into the chair on the far side. Her gaze met his, her eyes wide with alarm. He was worried himself. They could be interrupted at any moment. *You have to move. Get out of this building now, or you never will.*

He stood. The nurse sagged in her chair. He walked around the desk and stared down at her, and she looked up at him, her eyes wide. Two thoughts came to him. First, his plan to take her scrubs and walk out wasn't going to work. She was tiny.

Second, the fear in her eyes made it impossible. The thought of undressing her while she was helpless filled him with an unexpected shame. Whatever came next, he would leave her out of it.

The window didn't open, and the glass held a mesh of thin wires. He wouldn't be able to break it. He looked outside. Empty lawn stretched away, ending at a chain link fence with a parking lot on the far side. The sky was blue and dotted with small puffs of cloud. *This could be all I ever see of the outside world.* He tried to savour the moment, but anxiety was like a living thing inside him, thrashing, kicking at him, demanding that he move.

"What am I going to do?"

He looked at the nurse. By the expression on her face she, also, was preoccupied with the question of what he would do next.

"You're not helping." He looked around, searching for inspiration.

That was when he saw the jeans, folded neatly on a cardboard box behind the desk. A pair of shoes rested on the floor nearby. He found a blouse and got his arms into the sleeves, but the stitching tore when he lowered his elbows. By then, though, he'd spotted the coats.

There were three coats, one on the back of the desk chair and two more sharing a hook on a door he had never noticed in one corner. He figured the tiny denim jacket on the back of the chair belonged to the nurse. A garish pink coat hung on the door, and he considered it. It looked big enough, but it was hardly discreet.

Under the pink coat he found a scuffed leather bomber jacket. Made for someone quite stout, it hung loose on David's thin frame, the shoulder seams reaching halfway to his elbows. When he pushed the sleeves up they stayed above his wrists. It would do.

He opened the door and smiled. The office had a tiny bathroom. He checked his reflection in the little mirror over the sink. Zipping the jacket to his chin pretty much hid the blue pyjama top. He thought about the layout of the security station down the hall. There was a counter that would hide his slippered feet. He might get away with the blue pants.

He re-entered the office. The nurse had her desk phone in her hand, and she was staring at the number pad as if it was very far away. One finger stretched out, trembling and tentative.

"No!" He reached her in two quick steps, acting without thought. His fist lashed out and his knuckles smacked into the side of her face. Her head snapped to the side and she dropped the receiver.

He held the phone to his ear. Dial tone. He hung up.

The nurse put her cheek on the desk, arms curled protectively around her head. He stood over her, fists clenched, fighting a storm of conflicting emotion. Fury and terror and remorse chased themselves around inside his brain, and in the middle of it all he got distracted by the strangeness of it. Feelings were a novelty after so much time in the fog. The effect on his body was peculiar and fascinating, muscles tightening everywhere, his bladder suddenly demanding release.

The symptoms faded as he examined them. His breathing slowed, and he looked down at the nurse. "How long?" he said. He gestured at himself, at the surrounding walls. "How long have I been here? What happened to me?"

Her eyes closed and her arms went slack.

"Oh, for ...." David returned to the bathroom and scrutinized his reflection. He didn't look great. There weren't a lot of crowds he was likely to blend into. But for the couple of minutes he needed it might be enough.

The nurse opened her eyes when he grabbed her shoulders, straightened her up, and flopped her back in the chair. She giggled as he pushed the chair back.

He went through the desk drawers. There was little of value. He pocketed a pair of scissors without knowing why. Then he found a purse. His memories of the world outside were maddeningly vague, but credit cards sparked his interest. He took the cards, some twenty-dollar bills, and a handful of coins.

He looked at the nurse. A bit of coiling green cord went from a clip on her waistband to one pocket. He tugged on the cord and drew out a keychain and a magnetic card.

There was no way to know what else he might need. He would just have to march out and hope for the best.

He had one more preparation to make. Most of the patients had unmistakable body language. They slouched along, moving like zombies, heads down, shoulders curled forward, avoiding eye contact. No jacket could hide it.

David paced up and down in the nurse's office. He held his head up and pushed his shoulders back. After a minute he realized his arms were rigid at his sides and tried to relax them. He took longer and longer strides, experimenting with swinging his arms until he had a rhythm that felt right.

The nurse lifted her head, peered at him, then let her head sag back against the chair.

David moved into her bathroom and looked in the mirror. He frowned. He glared. Above all he made eye contact in the glass. Finally he settled on the relaxed, bored look he had seen on the face of his usual intern. *What was his name? I already forget. Not now. Concentrate.*

He added a slightly puckered brow, an expression he'd seen on the nurse's face while he talked about his dreams. It made him look more alert without needing a lot of concentration. He wanted to practice more, but he could no longer control his rising anxiety.

He left the bathroom, walked around the desk, and opened the office door.

A secretary moved past without seeing him. An orderly leaned against a doorjamb at the end of the hall. David stood frozen. After a breathless moment he stepped back into the office.

He picked up the nurse's tablet. The prop would lend him credibility. And it would fill his hands, keep him from fidgeting.

There was one last thing. A tiny coffee maker stood on a shelf behind the desk. There was perhaps a third of a cup of coffee in the little pot. He drained it with one swallow, and smiled.

David stepped back into the hall and started walking. *Head up. Eyes forward. Big steps. Oh, my God, I left the office door open. But I'm not going back.*

The corridor branched. To the right, the security checkpoint leading to the TV room and his bedroom. To the left, the unknown.

He turned left.

It took all his concentration to keep his legs from buckling. He had never seen this end of the corridor, never once turned his head to glance this way on all those bleary mornings. Along the walls were bright posters he didn't have time to examine. A young woman in a business suit smiled at him. A man in a lab coat hurried past.

David walked forward. Ahead was a set of heavy double doors, painted a tacky institutional green, and a card reader. *I am moving into the unknown. Oh God oh God oh God.*

He reached the double doors, fighting the urge to look over his shoulder. His hands plunged into the pockets of his jacket. He fumbled past the scissors, caught the card, and held it up to the reader.

He pushed the doors open.

And froze briefly in the doorway. There was another door straight ahead and a security booth to his right. The bored guard was just starting to look up.

David recovered his presence of mind just in time and stepped forward. If he was up close to the guard's window, the man couldn't see his pyjama pants and slippers.

Thick wire mesh covered a window in the top half of the next door. David touched the mesh. The walls beyond were splashed with sunlight.

"Excuse me."

David jumped. The guard was staring at him. David gaped, then remembered his "bored intern" expression. He puckered his brow and looked at the man.

The guard was very young, a plump man with a brush cut. "You forgot to sign out."

David hunted briefly with his eyes, then found a thick book on the counter beside him. He took up the pen, didn't even try to understand the photocopied form he saw, and made illegible marks in all the blanks the last person had filled in.

"It's nine fourteen."

David dutifully printed "9:14" in the last blank. He was sure there was something he should say to the guard now. Some sort of social pleasantry.

Instead he dropped the pen, turned mutely to the door, and pushed. A buzzer sounded and the door opened.

David stepped through into a foyer with boot racks and another window into the security booth. Before him he saw a set of double doors, these ones ordinary clear glass, with a sidewalk and a blue sky visible beyond.

He didn't pause. He barely saw the room around him as he hurried to the glass doors, shoved them open, and stepped outside.

Images came to him so quickly he could barely register them. Sunshine, trees, green green grass and rows of parked cars, people walking toward him across the parking lot, and beneath it all a torrent of fractured pictures from his memory, none of it making sense.

Panic crashed over him and put his feet into motion at a pace just short of a run. He crossed a parking lot, reached a fence, and spent a moment just clutching the wire. An engine growled and a car door slammed, making him flinch. He smelled exhaust and oil, asphalt and dirt. The sun was too bright, the noises too harsh after the insulated world he'd just left.

He squinted, reducing the world to streaks of light and dark. His fingers squeezed the cold wire of the fence. Beneath the rumble of car engines and the distant honk of a horn he heard birdsong. He smelled grass and leaves. A breeze cooled his skin, blunting the keen edge of his terror.

You have to move. The rest of the world was still too much to take in, so he focussed on the fence. Wire diamonds dragged against his fingers as he walked. He followed the fence until he came to an opening and moved through onto a sidewalk. He crossed a street, only thinking to look for traffic when he was on the far side. Buildings loomed behind more chain link fences. He was in an industrial park, with a lot of open space and cluttered storage yards.

He walked. He walked for blocks, turning frequently, and lost all sense of direction. It was the most exercise he'd had in a long time, and his breath sawed in his chest.

At last the worst of the fear subsided. His steps slowed, and when he saw a bench he sat down. *This is a bus stop. I know what a bus stop is. So I wasn't always in an institution.*

Well, who the hell am I, then?

He rested his legs and let his mind stop racing. Time passed. He put a hand in the pocket of his stolen jacket.

The first thing he encountered was the scissors. *What else do I have?* Credit cards. Bills. Coins. He put the coins in a careful pile beside his leg. It looked like two or three bucks. He put the credit cards and the paper money back in his pocket.

Then he picked up the scissors. He knew pretty much why he had taken everything else. But why the scissors?

They were for the security guard. He might have tried to stop you. You use the scissors. It's easy. It works because the other person doesn't expect it.

He flinched at the thought and put the scissors on the bench beside him. He pushed them away. But then he picked them up and replaced them in his pocket. *Someone else might try to stop me.*

Four

At last a bus came. David dropped his pile of change into the opening, took a transfer, and sat down with no idea where he was going or what to do next. He hadn't expected to get this far.

When the bus stopped in front of a shopping mall he got off and walked inside. A department store caught his eye. He got jeans and a t-shirt and headed for a checkout counter. He was counting out cash when he remembered the credit cards. He fumbled out a Visa card, spent a panicky moment trying to remember how credit cards worked, and finally just pushed it across the counter to the check-out girl.

She slid it back to him. "You can tap."

He stared at her, mystified, and she gestured at a card reader on the counter. Finally she took the card from him and touched it to the reader. "There you go. Would you like a receipt?"

"Um, no." He grabbed his possessions and hurried out.

Another store sold him running shoes. He changed in the men's room and wadded his pyjamas and slippers into the garbage. *Should I throw the jacket away? Will they be looking for a man in a brown jacket?* There were enough pockets in the jeans for the money and credit cards.

He looked at the scissors. *Why was I locked up? Did I hurt someone?* He remembered the dream with his hands covered in blood, and his stomach roiled.

He kept the jacket, but he left the scissors on the bathroom counter.

The sights and sounds and smells of the mall brought back a jumble of half-formed memories. He tried to extract something concrete, then gave up and let his mind wander.

They will try to catch me. If I hurt someone, they'll try very hard. They will trace the credit cards, but it will take time. How long? he wondered. *A few days? Hours? Do they even know I'm missing yet?*

He walked through the mall, trying to shrug off a growing tension. He had no idea how long he'd be free, so he should enjoy every moment, right?

But paranoia crawled into his skull and sped his steps. The nausea he'd felt in the bathroom lingered and grew worse. He told himself he was overreacting. He took deep breaths. None of it helped.

He was almost running by the time he burst out of the mall. Sunlight slammed into his eyes. How could people stand such searing light, endlessly pouring out of the sky? David squinted against the glare and walked, almost blind.

When sirens blared behind him he jumped. He stood frozen, adrenalin flooding his bloodstream, then told himself to calm down. *For all you know it's an ambulance or a fire truck. Nothing to do with you.*

A second siren started up, then a third. With a massive effort of will David made himself take a casual step forward, then another. A police car went past, lights flashing, and he turned to watch.

The car pulled into the parking lot of the mall.

Don't run. He clung to the thought, even as his body demanded that he flee. *You're completely ordinary. Just some guy on the street. Impossible to notice. Unless you run.*

A quick glance around told him he was on the sidewalk beside a pretty major road. A narrow residential street beckoned to his right, and he turned, walking briskly. The last of the sirens went silent and he rubbed sweating palms against his t-shirt, fighting for calm.

When they don't find me in the mall they'll cruise the streets. His eyes darted from side to side, looking for a place to hide. He thought about slipping into someone's back yard, even took a few steps across a lawn before a barking dog sent him scampering back. *Quit attracting attention. Just walk.*

A block later he reached a strip mall. He was heading for a convenience store, wondering how long he could pretend to browse the aisles, when he spotted a tiny café and changed direction. He plunged inside, out of the harsh glare of the sun, out of sight from the street, and immediately felt better.

"Hi!" The girl behind the counter gave him a bright smile, and for a terrible moment David thought she recognized him. He stared at her until her smile started to slip, then gathered himself and looked away. He was the only customer. He tried to read the chalkboards above her, but the words dropped out of his mind as quickly as he read them.

"Um, hi." He walked up to the counter, giving her a quick glance. Her smile was back in place. "Um, do you serve breakfast?"

"Sure do!" She rattled off half a dozen breakfast options, too fast for David to follow.

"That last one," he said. "With the bagel?"

"You bet! Would you like coffee with that?"

For the first time, a bit of enthusiasm replaced some of the worry in David's mind. "I would love a coffee."

"Great." She listed half a dozen coffee options, speaking like she was in some kind of race. David stared at her helplessly, and her professional smile became something more sympathetic. "Just a regular coffee?"

He nodded.

"Coming right up."

He paid cash, then sat down with a steaming cup. He wanted to fidget. Hell, he wanted to get up and pace. Instead, he grabbed a newspaper from another table. He couldn't read it, but it kept his hands occupied.

The masthead said "Red Deer Advocate". David stared at the three words, convinced that an important memory was just a hair's breadth away. *I'm in a place called Red Deer. I know that name. It's ....*

The girl set a plate in front of him, and the almost-memory vanished. David took a bite of toasted bagel filled with scrambled egg. His queasy stomach protested, settling somewhat when he swallowed. He ate, barely tasting the food. Then he sipped his coffee and pretended to read the newspaper.

A police car went past, moving slowly. David turned the page and looked at pictures of football players and watched the street from the corner of his eye while he waited for his pulse to return to normal.

The last inch of coffee was cold in the bottom of his cup when a train whistle blew, close enough to be uncomfortably loud. He squeezed his eyes shut, feeling the eggs shift in his stomach.

When he opened his eyes, he knew what to do.

The train tracks were a block from the café. A freight train stood there, not moving, and David stared at it, trying to think through a haze of nausea and fear. He'd imagined rectangular boxcars with sliding doors, but the graffiti-splashed cars before him were fat cylinders, sloping outward at each end. Beneath the slope was a little platform where a person might crouch and catch a discreet ride.

Metal squealed, the entire train gave a jerk, and it started to move. David walked toward it, his heart thumping. The sun was to his left, and he lifted a hand to shade his eyes.

And stopped, thinking. *It must be close to noon. Which means the sun is ... south?* It was frustratingly difficult to dredge up something so fundamental. *This is a northbound train. That's the wrong way.*

He had no idea why he was suddenly sure he wanted to go south, but he decided not to question it. He watched the train creep past, doing his best to look bored and insignificant when a couple of pickup trucks pulled up to the crossing to wait. The last train car finally passed and he walked across the tracks. When the miniature traffic jam cleared, he turned and walked parallel to the rails. He found a shady spot against the blank back wall of a building and sat down to wait.

Despite the tension, despite his roiling stomach, he fell asleep. A train whistle woke him and he watched a couple of locomotives lurch past, moving slower and slower. A dozen or so flatbed rail cars went by, then more of the cylindrical cars. When twenty or thirty cars passed at a brisk walking pace he decided the train wasn't going to stop. He got up, looked toward the locomotives, and saw they were hidden by a bend in the track.

Well, here goes nothing. He jogged beside the train, caught a metal ladder at the back of a car, and clambered up. There was a grubby platform behind the ladder, and he sat down cross-legged, the back of his head touching the sloped end of the container. Winded by the brief exertion, he sagged over, lying on his side. *Wow, I'm really out of shape.*

Compared to what? Once again his memory refused to give him any context. He was trying to figure out how he knew what "out of shape" meant when he fell asleep.

The train lurched to a halt, feet clattered on the ladder, and strong hands closed on David's ankles. Burly cops dragged him down and shoved him onto his stomach on the ground. David thrashed, groping for the scissors, but the cops grabbed his wrists and pulled his arms back until handcuffs cut into his flesh. Someone bashed him across the head with a nightstick, and in a dark corner of his mind David thought, *I deserve this*.

The nightmare faded and his limbs relaxed. He sat on a stool, one elbow resting on a bar of dark polished wood. Soft music played in the background, interwoven with murmuring voices.

"Here you go." A dark-haired man with a genial smile set a coaster in front of David, then covered it with a glass of amber liquid. Moisture beaded the glass, slicking David's fingers as he picked it up. He smacked his lips and lifted the glass, watching tiny bubbles rise to the surface and burst. He sniffed. *Beer. Nice and malty, too.* He lifted the glass to his lips.

"Remember," said the bartender. "You have to have a way to leave."

David froze, the beer a tantalizing half-inch from his lips. "What?"

The man gave him a knowing look. "If you don't have a way to leave, you'll just keep doing the same thing forever."

"What does that even mean?"

The bartender shrugged. "You should know. It's the first thing you taught me."

"What? What do you—"

But the bartender was already gone, the bar as well. David brought the glass to his lips, too late. He held only mist.

I want my .... He frowned and looked at his hands, sure he'd lost something and unable to remember what. He looked around, trying to jog his memory.

He stood on some sort of concrete platform with benches shaded by trees in pots. Before him a green city stretched out, a vista of rooftops and trees. Beyond that he could make out a cluster of skyscrapers and a round tower.

The backdrop for the entire scene was a row of enchanting blue mountains stretching across the horizon. Young sharp peaks, snow-capped and gilded by sun. The sky overhead was blue and cloudless, tinged with pink as sunset neared.

He held someone's hand. He couldn't seem to turn his head to look at her, but he knew who she was. She was slim and graceful and beautiful, and she loved him. In fact, they were in love, with the easy familiarity of two people who share trust and friendship as well as infatuation.

A sense of well-being suffused him. His mind was clear of drugs, and his memory, although no specific memories emerged, was clear, complete, undamaged.

He was peripherally aware of his body, relaxed and strong and tanned, and his stance. He stood tall and confident beside his lover, unafraid, free of shadows. He was a whole, complete man.

The train lurched, the steel plate beneath him gave him a thump, and David woke up. He lay curled in a fetal position, his muscles cramped, his head aching. He rolled onto his back and looked around.

Open farmland stretched to the horizon, the dark soil showing hints of green. The train moved so slowly he could have jumped to the ground and run alongside.

The cold metal beneath him chilled him. He zipped up his jacket, moved to the sunny side of his little platform, and stretched out with his fingers laced behind his head. Even with a headache and an upset stomach, the memory of his dream made it impossible to feel unhappy.

A hawk moved in a lazy circle high above, and David nodded, telling himself they were two of a kind. *Wild and free. That's us.* The past was a hazy tangle, the future was too bleak to think about, but in this moment the world belonged to him.

I've seen this view before. He twisted his head around and looked across the fields beside the tracks. *Not from a train, maybe. But I've seen it. Through a car window, I think. I was a passenger. I was bored. Nothing to do but watch the countryside go past.*

No details came to him, but the mist that hid the past felt thinner than ever before. He would remember everything soon. He was sure of it. It was there, barely out of reach.

Warmed by the sun, soothed by the repetitive clatter of the steel wheels beneath him, David drifted into sleep and remembered the first really important day of his life.

Five

Autumn leaves hung mischievously over the city's still-pristine lawns as September came to a close. David's eighth birthday was coming up, and he was very excited.

He was hoping for a BMX bike, like Josh Wilson had. He was pretty sure he wouldn't get one, because Dad had explained last year and the year before that it would be frivolous for a youngest child to get a brand-new bike. Dad had an older brother, and had never gotten a brand-new bike in his life. He rode his brother's hand-me-downs, and so David would ride the bikes his brother Matthew and his sister Emily had outgrown. Dad had explained that these values were very important for David to learn, so he wouldn't be spoiled.

But still, David clung to a faint hope. When his parents called him into the kitchen a week before the big day, he expected to hear the annual lecture about new bikes.

"David", his Mom said, "this year your birthday falls on a Saturday. We thought you might want to do something special that day. How would you like to spend your birthday?"

When David cried, "Can we go to Grandpa's?" his father scowled and his mother's forehead furrowed. But when David's face fell, they both made fake-looking smiles and told him, "Sure".

In the past, David's mother had arranged birthday parties for him, with three or four kids from his class invited over. This, however, was the first year David had been consulted on the matter. He felt very grown-up as he made his decision. He saw his classmates every day, and the truth was, he didn't really like them all that much. Even his friends could suddenly turn mean and make fun of him for no reason. He wouldn't miss them on his birthday. But a trip to Grandpa's was something special.

David's memories of his grandparents were vague. He hadn't seen them in two years, fully a quarter of his lifetime. But his recollections, though fuzzy, were all beautiful. He could picture the farm, with a white and green house standing alone in an impossibly wide yard, and some ducks in a pen. The little duck pond was a lake in his memory, the ducks alarmingly big. But in his mind's eye the sun was always bright, the air full of perfume and adventure, and his grandfather a kindly paragon who gave David his undivided attention.

Grandma lived there too, of course, but in David's mind she was a vague, foolish figure who made her voice high and cute whenever she spoke to him. It was Grandpa, who treated him like an equal, that David really wanted to see.

Over the next few days some tension crept into the household. Every time the subject of his birthday came up, David's father would frown and mutter, and his mother made a half-hearted attempt to talk him out of it, saying wouldn't it be nice to have his friends over?

The tension made David uneasy, but he was distracted by excitement at the prospect of seeing Grandpa again. So he ignored his father's dark looks and his own anxieties, and smiled and shook his head at his mother's suggestions. And at last his birthday arrived.

The morning brought bright sunshine and high stripes of cloud, which glowed with gold like David's memories of the farm. Mom seemed genuinely happy, looking forward to the excursion. Even Dad displayed a hearty, if phoney, cheerfulness, although from time to time his face grew long and he would fidget.

Emily and Matthew, one and a half and two and a half years older than David, sat silently in the back seat for the whole trip, looking out the windows and not speaking. David sat between them, chattering and pointing. Mom reached back to caress his hair, Dad smiled indulgently, and the car moved out of the city.

The farm was perhaps half an hour beyond the city limits. Mom pointed at blocks of new houses and told them solemnly that she could remember when this had all been farmland. Dad was quiet, occasionally drumming his fingers on the steering wheel.

At last the car crested a hill and the farm came into view. David's heart leapt, and he surged forward against his seatbelt. The big square house was weather-beaten but newer than the barn, and the yard, though well-maintained, was populated mostly by dust and very old trucks. But to David it was the stuff of a dream. He had been struggling for a week to remember things he hadn't seen since he was five, and now the images were falling into place. He was intoxicated.

The car seemed to slow down now that the farm was in sight, and a sigh made David glance to his left. His father's eyes stared off into the distance.

They turned into the long driveway.

A pair of dogs, a collie and some sort of chunky red mongrel, erupted around the corner of the house and threw themselves at the car, barking madly. And the door of the house opened, and Grandpa came out.

He looked exactly as David remembered him, exactly as a farmer ought to look. He wore a red plaid shirt and jeans, with suspenders holding them in place. His hands and face were burned dark brown from the sun, with a pale stripe showing at the wrists. His hair was like the stuffing in a teddy bear, soft-looking and curly and white. He wore a worried frown, but as soon as the car came close, the old man's face split into a wide smile.

The dogs snarled and slavered until Dad opened his car door. Then they were magically transformed, crowding forward with wagging tails to jump up on the visitors and lick faces and hands. Grandpa, laughing, pushed at the dogs while apologizing, and led them to the house.

Grandma met them at the front door, brushing floury

hands on a flowery apron and explaining that she was cooking, fluttering her arms in excitement and urging them into the kitchen. "Goodness," she said, "I was starting to think you folks would never visit again."

Dad gave her a sharp glance, and Grandpa winced. Grandma looked around uncertainly, then fled to the fridge, where she rummaged vigorously for refreshments, chatting about baking and how she'd made fruit punch.

The rest of them sat around the kitchen table for the better part of two minutes, making awkward conversation. The palpable tension, plus an unexpected shyness, made David silent. He put his elbows on the tabletop and gazed anxiously at the adults.

Grandpa, in the middle of a rather dull story about one of his trucks, let his voice trickle off, and looked around in the cool silence that followed. His gaze rested on David with a pensive expression. Then he smiled broadly and clapped his hands together. "So! Who'd like a tour of the farm?"

All of David's nervous energy returned in a rush, and he bounded up. The rest of the family rose too, visibly relieved. Grandma stayed behind to mind her baking while everyone else trouped outside.

The dogs were driven back with shoves and good-natured insults, and the six of them hiked across the yard. They toured the pens, and David threw fists full of grain to chickens, turkeys and ducks in turn. He found the chickens a bit dull, the turkeys comical, and the ducks cute to the point of distraction. Only when the wind began to blow cold past the duck pen did he finally turn away, to the relief of everyone else.

Back in the house, Grandma was checking a pie. She fussed and chattered while she opened the oven, muttering a bad word when she burned her thumb. She told them it would be another few minutes, and began setting the table.

Grandpa, his eyes twinkling, said, "Did you want to see your present, David?"

David sat bolt upright, then popped out of his chair. He had forgotten all about presents!

He bounced down the hall behind Grandpa, Dad and Mom in his wake. Grandpa stopped at a bedroom door and grinned. "You'll have to forgive us for not wrapping it, but you see .... Took me all day to get it assembled properly." He swung the door open with a flourish, stepping quickly through and to one side. David and his parents crowded in.

It was a bike. A BMX. Brand new, the right size, shiny and red and so beautiful it made David's chest ache. He leaped forward, then stopped short, hesitant. Finally he reached out, slowly, and touched the rubber grip on the handlebar. He was dimly aware that he was bouncing on the balls of his feet and smiling so hard his face hurt.

Grandpa looked at him. "Do you like it?"

"Oh, Grandpa—" The bike was wonderful, and tied in with all his anticipation of this day, all his missing of Grandpa. David's eyes stung, and he surged forward in a quick, spontaneous leap. He threw his arms around Grandpa, something he'd wanted to do all along, but he'd been too shy. Tears poured down his cheeks, and he just screwed his eyes shut and squeezed the old man.

There was a hand now on the top of David's head, gently ruffling his hair, and Grandpa's voice was husky as he said, "Aw, shucks, son ...." David would never have done such a thing with his father; Dad wasn't that kind of person. But he sensed Grandpa didn't mind.

Then hard fingers sank into David's shoulder and dragged him backward. His arms came reluctantly loose from Grandpa, and he looked up.

Dad's face was stony and cold, his mouth set. He glared at David, one lip beginning to curl. "You can't keep the bike."

David stared at his father. He blinked away the last few tears, felt a tickle of mucus at his nostrils, and was too scared to sniff or wipe it.

It was Grandpa who finally said, in a mild voice, "Why?" But Dad stared into David's face as he answered.

"It's frivolous and unnecessary. Matthew's old bike is perfectly good."

Then no one spoke or moved, and the moment stretched out, impossibly painful for David, who was confused and filled with a nameless fear. He felt as if he had somehow betrayed his father, hurt him terribly to provoke this angry reaction. But he couldn't figure out what he had done wrong.

When he couldn't stand another second of it, and his mouth was opening to release some sort of inarticulate scream, Grandma appeared in the doorway and chirped, "The pie's done!" She glanced around at the taut, shocked faces, smiled in incomprehension, and said, "Do you like the bike, David?"

The fingers sank deeper into David's shoulder. Then abruptly Dad released him and stepped without a word past Grandma and into the hall. The others, silent, filed past the old woman and followed the smell of baking to the kitchen. She smiled uncertainly and followed them.

After the pie was eaten, Matthew, desperate for some distraction, dug out an ancient set of plastic soldiers. David, numb, joined his brother and sister for a lacklustre game in a corner of the living room.

After five minutes of moving little plastic men back and forth, David found he could concentrate no longer. The bike kept floating before his eyes, terrible in its new importance. It had become a symbol, of Grandpa's love, of Dad's anger, of David's new age.

He supposed he would never see the bike again, though he knew he would never forget it. He stared sightlessly at the green infantryman in his fist, then decided he would take one last look at the beautiful bike. Then he could get on with the chore of forgetting this awful birthday.

He set the toy down and stood up. Mom and Grandma sat in the kitchen, backs to him, sipping coffee and speaking quietly. Dad and Grandpa were not in sight.

David stepped into the hall, Matt and Emily watching him silently. The bedroom door was half open. Fearful of his father's reaction if he saw him, David crept forward and peered around the door.

Dad and Grandpa stood in the room. Their attention

was focussed entirely on each other, and they didn't see David. They were speaking, in cold, hard voices, saying things that the watching boy didn't really understand. But the words stuck like nettles in his mind, where he would review them hundreds of times in the future.

Dad swore in a brittle voice that barely carried to the boy in the doorway. There was urgency in his stance, something like pleading in his face, but cold harshness in his voice. His eyes were fixed on Grandpa as he cursed.

Finally Dad's tirade wore down. He stood for a moment glaring, yet strangely vulnerable. Then he spoke, just a little more calmly.

"You stupid bastard. Do you have any idea what a shitty father you were? And now you're trying to buy my son's love, and take away his respect for me—"

"Sam." It startled David to hear his father's given name. Even Mom just called him Dad. "Son, I know I let you down. But I can't change it. By the time I saw my mistakes, it was too late. You were all grown up, and you already hated me.

"But forget about this stupid bike for a minute, and forget about me. I want you to think about David. The way you treat him is no better than the way I treated you. Maybe it's too late for us, but it's not too late for you and David."

Dad's face darkened, and his voice crackled. "If you think that buying a bike now—"

"Listen to me!" There was an unexpected strength in Grandpa's voice. "This isn't about me. This is about you and David. What's going to happen when he's your age?

What'll happen when you talk to David as a man? Will it be like this? Will he hate you like you hate me? That's something you have to decide now."

Dad's hand shot out, and he grabbed a fist full of Grandpa's shirt, pulling him close. With their noses an inch apart he began to snarl. "*You* are talking to *me* about parenting? You are the stupidest, meanest, most idiotic and half-baked, manipulative, selfish, insensitive—"

David burst into the room. He stretched to reach Dad's arm, grabbed it and wailed, "No! No, stop it!"

Dad gave Grandpa a shove that sent the old man stumbling back. He tripped on the bike, falling and knocking it over. David immediately let go of Dad's arm and ran to Grandpa. It looked like Grandpa was all right, gathering himself to stand. Tears poured down David's face, and he sobbed, with no idea what to do. He said, "I'm sorry, Grandpa. It'll be okay."

The old man stared past him, but murmured, "Okay, David."

Then fingers sank into David's shoulder again, and Dad sent him reeling toward the door. Dad yelled, "Get out!", and David obeyed, bumping the door frame because he was blinded by tears. He ran down the hall, rebounded from the wall, hurtled through the kitchen and outside.

He stood outside the duck pen and cried and shook, facing the ducks but unable see them. When he couldn't stand the cold anymore he turned around. Across the yard he saw Matthew and Emily getting into the car. Mom stood with Grandma and Grandpa on the porch, none of them speaking.

Then Dad came out of the house carrying the bike. He opened the trunk, put the bike in, and closed the trunk with a bungee cord. He turned and scanned the yard, spotted David.

"David! Get in the car."

David plodded across the yard. Mom and Dad got into the car, and the engine started. One back door was open for David.

He looked at Grandma and Grandpa as he walked past. Grandpa's face solemn, but he smiled at David. David tried to smile back, but failed.

He got in the car without saying goodbye.

They drove in silence up the driveway and turned onto a gravel road. David knew he'd somehow hurt his father. He didn't know yet that Dad never would forgive him.

About a mile from the farm, Dad stopped the car. He got out, walked around to the trunk, took out the BMX, and threw it into the ditch. Then he closed the trunk, got back behind the wheel, and drove away.

David looked down at his shoes and tried to think about the ducks and how cute they'd been.

No one spoke on the drive home.

Six

A train whistle blew, and David opened his eyes. He shivered, rubbing his chilly hands together as he sat up. He stared around, disoriented.

Houses rolled past on the far side of a chain-link fence. *This must be Calgary.* He stood, then put a hand on his stomach, leaning over while he waited for his gut to unclench.

When he straightened he saw the arm of a traffic barrier a few feet away. Cars were lined up on the other side, waiting for the train to pass. He froze, cursing himself for standing. *I'm in plain sight. Someone will report me. They'll send me back.*

As soon as the intersection was out of sight he jumped off. The train wasn't moving fast, but he landed sprawling, bruising his palms. The fence had resumed. He staggered to the wire, made a half-hearted attempt to climb, then gave up and trudged along, waiting for a gap.

At a cross-street he left the tracks, stepping onto a sidewalk. More train tracks ran parallel to the first set, and he followed them with his eyes to a concrete platform.

CTrain. He examined the word, puzzling out the meaning. *It's a commuter train. It goes downtown.*

Without a better idea, he walked to the platform and sagged onto a bench. When a train arrived he boarded it and stared out the window as buildings went by.

Several stops later he stood up. He didn't know why, but his legs seemed to know what they were doing, so he let them take over. He left the train and rode up an escalator, then walked across a pedestrian bridge over a busy road. He kept experiencing flashes of almost-recognition that would fade before he could pull out a full-blown memory. By the time he plodded down a staircase to street level he was frustrated and grouchy, with knots beginning to form in the muscles of his shoulders

This is Macleod Trail. He scowled at the road beside him. *I can't remember my own last name, but I remember the name of this stupid street.* He turned in a slow circle. Whatever tendril of memory had guided him this far was gone. Nothing looked remotely familiar.

The steady flow of traffic on Macleod chipped away at his nerves, driver after driver getting a good look at him as they went past. He put his back to the busy road and marched up a quiet cross street, squinting at the sky. The sun was below the nearest rooftops.

It's still early morning. He shook his head, then winced as pain sloshed through his skull. *It can't be. It must be late afternoon. I should have bought a watch. Or taken one from that nurse.*

He was glad he hadn't, though. He wanted to resent her for helping keep him locked up and tranquillized, but righteous indignation eluded him. *Nurses are good people, aren't they? Professional helpers. She probably thought she was doing the right thing.*

Maybe she was right. After all, look what you did as soon as you missed a few doses. You poisoned her. You stole.

No, he protested to the cold voice. *I only did what I had to. I only gave her the same drugs she gave me.*

You gave her a huge dose. She probably died.

No! He brought both hands up, rubbing his temples. *The place is full of doctors and nurses. I'm sure she was fine. I didn't do anything very bad.*

You trespassed on railway property.

That last thought was so absurd he gave a low snort of laughter. Laughing felt good, and so strange that his conscience relented. *They took laughter away from me. And everything else. I have a right to get it back.*

He walked. He had no destination, but each time he slowed, his stomach would twist like a wet towel being wrung out. He couldn't tell if it was withdrawal or plain anxiety, but it faded when his feet moved.

So he walked.

A memory came to him, of perspiration slicking his skin while his feet made a steady pattering sound against an asphalt pathway. He walked a bit faster, trying to tease out more of that memory. Finally he started to run.

In three blocks he was fighting for breath. But the movement of his legs, regular as a metronome, soothed his mind. He forced himself to go on, a little more slowly. The more his legs and lungs strained, the more his mind relaxed, and the swirl of formless memories triggered by the city became clearer.

I used to be a runner.

He sensed if he could keep this up long enough he would break through into a painless rhythm, his body releasing endorphins that would fill him with serenity.

But a knifing pain in his side made him stagger, and he stopped, panting. By the time he caught his breath another memory came to him. *Cooldown.* He resumed walking, using long, swinging steps so his legs wouldn't stiffen.

Where can I go? I need help. Someone to take me in, hide me until I can clear my head. He thought of Emily. His strongest memory of his sister was her exaggerated sighs when she had to interact with him. She had preferred to pretend he didn't exist. To be fair, this behaviour was pretty much mutual.

Well, what about Matthew? No, wait. Matt's dead. Isn't he? He shuddered. *How can I forget something like that?* The image of a hospital corridor flashed through his mind, Mom distraught, Dad as cold and expressionless as a rock. David watching, until an orderly tugged on his arm. "Come on. Dinner time. There'll be jello."

No, that's not right. He struggled to bring back the hospital, but the harder he tried, the more it blended with the institution, the memories tangling until he couldn't tell which was which.

He was trudging along, eyes on the concrete just ahead of his toes, when he saw a square drawn in bright blue chalk. Beyond that were two more squares, one red and one green, and more beyond those. David put his left foot in the blue square, hopped, and landed with a foot in each of the next two squares. He hopped and bounced to the end of the grid, then stopped, feeling inexplicably cheerful.

The hopscotch grid gave way to random bits of chalk art. He admired a stick figure drawn in orange, then a house in a garish blend of colours. A bright yellow sun caught his eye, complete with a smiling face and radiating sunbeams. He squatted, examining the drawing. *It's not right. It should be ... less symmetrical. It should mean something.*

He straightened up. *'Mean something'? What the hell does that mean?* He stared at the yellow circle, letting his eyes go out of focus. *I knew someone who used to draw on the sidewalk with chalk.*

This is stupid. He turned, resumed walking. *I don't need to remember my lame childhood. I need a family member, a friend. Someone who can help me.*

The image of the chalk wouldn't leave him, though. *I made fun of him, but the truth is, it was beautiful.* He could almost see it, a circle made of graceful, incomprehensible calligraphy, the roughness of chalk on asphalt not quite robbing it of its elegance. *Even if they had just been abstract pictures, I would have been impressed. But each one was a poem.*

A shadowy figure seemed to crouch in the corner of David's eye, holding a piece of chalk as thick as a good cigar. When David tried to bring him into sharper focus he turned into one of the orderlies in the institution.

"Damn it." David shoved his hands in his pockets, annoyed. His thoughts kept looping, running in pointless circles, and the more he tried to remember, the worse it got. Around and around and around it went, until he wanted to scream in frustration.

If you don't have a way to leave, you'll just keep doing the same thing forever.

And just like that, he remembered.

"Hey, chicken lips!"

David pretended not to hear as someone clucked noisily behind him. He wasn't sure where his nickname had come from, but someone saddled him with it in the tenth grade and it had stuck with him for two more years. The sound faded as he reached his locker.

"Yo." A dark-haired boy with a crooked nose spun the dial on a padlock a few lockers down. "David, right?"

David looked suspiciously at him, a short guy with the solid build of a wrestler. *It's that new kid.* The boy's smile seemed friendly enough. *He doesn't know about me yet. What's his name?*

"Mohammed?"

"Moe." The boy stuck a fist out. David hesitated, then gave him a knuckle bump.

"You're that crazy runner," said Moe. "You lapped me, like, three times in PE." He seemed genuinely admiring. "How do you do it?"

David's cheeks warmed. "I like running."

Moe peered closely at him. "You're lying."

"Well." David shrugged. "I like that it's straightforward. All you need are shoes and a little determination." *And you can be alone when you run.*

"Say, do you get that Computer Lit stuff?"

David nodded, relieved by the change in subject. "Yeah, pretty much. You?"

"Hell, no." Moe sighed theatrically as he dumped books in his locker, took out a paper bag, and locked up. "As soon as we started loops I was lost. They don't make sense!"

"Sure they do." David grabbed his own lunch, then closed his locker, thinking. "It's like PE. Say Jones tells us to run ten laps around the gym. He's not going to say, run a lap, then run another lap, then run a third lap, and so on. He's going to say, run ten laps, right?"

"Yes," said Moe sadly. "Because he's a heartless monster."

David laughed. "They're just laps. Ten isn't so bad."

"Not for you." Moe balanced on one foot, sticking out a thick leg. "Look how short my legs are!" They started down the hallway, walking side by side. "I know. It's like those, what do you call them? 'For' loops. When you have to do something ten times."

"For i equals one to ten," David said.

"Yeah. That." Moe made an irritated gesture, then muttered a curse when his lunch bag almost spilled. "So why do we need the other kind?"

"Well, sometimes you don't know how many times to loop." David pointed at the hallway ahead. "Like right now. I'm way too tired to watch where I'm going. So I'm going to tell my brain, just keep walking until you're outside."

Moe gave him a skeptical, amused look. "Right."

"Do while sunshine equals zero," said David. "Lift your foot. Swing your leg forward. Put your foot down. Loop. Nothing to it."

"Sure," said Moe. "What could be easier?"

"Actually, I missed a step. The last thing in a loop should always be a way to get out of the loop. If you don't have a way to leave, you'll just keep doing the same thing forever."

"Sounds like my mom," Moe quipped. He looked genuinely interested, though, so David continued.

"Do while sunshine equals zero. Take a step. Look around. Loop. 'Look around' is where you find out if sunshine is still zero." He thought for a moment. "I'll start another loop when we get outside. I want to eat and shoot the shit until twelve thirty. So the start of the loop would be ...?"

Moe frowned. "Do ... while ... it's not twelve thirty?"

"Sure. Or, say, do while time is less than twelve thirty. Then, inside the loop, you have some commands. One. Take a bite of sandwich. Two. Think up a good 'yo mama is so fat' joke. Three. Insult Moe's mother."

That made Moe laugh. He held up a hand before David could speak again. "Loop, to loop back." He scrunched his face up, concentrating. "But first, that other thing you said. You need a way to get out of the loop. So you look at your phone or something. Check the time. Otherwise you'll be ragging on my mother forever."

"I'm sure she's a nice lady," David said. "But she could lose a few pounds."

Someone clucked loudly behind them, and a girl giggled. David gritted his teeth and ignored it.

Moe, oblivious, peered into his lunch bag with the air of a janitor investigating a plugged toilet. "I think my mom is stuck in a loop. One where she makes me the same thing every day." He gave David a speculative look. "Do you like Persian food?"

David stopped himself from asking if it was like Mexican food and instead said, "I don't know."

"So, a fifty percent chance, then. I'm a hundred percent sure I'm tired of Persian food, which I eat several times a day, every day of my life. Mathematically, that means we should trade." He looked at David's lunch bag. "What have you got?"

"Bologna and cheese sandwich."

Moe raised a thick black eyebrow. "Is there pork in the bologna?"

"There could be anything in the bologna. I try not to think about it." David dug in his lunch bag. "I've got a grape jelly sandwich and a bottle of orange juice."

A boy pushed past from behind, giving David a shoulder check that sent him stumbling into Moe. His name was Brad, and if he wasn't David's only tormentor, he was probably the worst one. Several more students went past, laughing, as Moe helped David regain his balance.

"Dicks," Moe said, watching them push open the doors at the end of the hall and vanish into the sunshine. To David he said, "I call dibs on the jelly sandwich. I can offer you a choice of chicken kebabs or rice cake." He held up a warning finger. "The chicken sounds better, but my mother does terrible things to chicken when she cooks. I think she must have been badly pecked as a child. I recommend the rice cake."

They reached the doors, pushed them open, and stepped outside.

"Think fast, chicken lips!" Brad and his friends were on the stairs outside, leaning on the railings. As David went past, Brad slapped the bag out of his hand.

The bag hit concrete, glass broke, and a pool of orange juice spread outward. Something hit David from behind, and he stumbled down the steps. As he reached the bottom, another impact knocked him to his knees.

Brad landed face-down on the sidewalk beside him, face blank with shock. His body jerked, his face scrunched up, and he let out a grunt of pain.

David scrambled to his feet. The other kids still leaned on the railings, frozen, eyes wide, staring. Moe, his face a snarl, stood over Brad.

"You stupid fuck." Moe drove a hard kick into Brad's side. "Asshole." Another kick. "Piece of shit."

With the next kick, Brad rolled into a ball, arms protecting his ribs. Moe circled around, lined up a toe with the back of Brad's head, and drew back his foot.

"Moe!"

Moe gave David a startled look, his rage fading for a moment.

"That's enough. Come on."

Moe's face collapsed back into a vicious scowl. "There's only one way these fuckers learn." His foot started to swing.

David lunged forward, leaning across Brad's curled body, both palms hitting Moe's chest. He shoved, as hard as he could. It was like slapping a brick wall. Moe was solid muscle. Still, the impact pushed him back a step, interrupting his kick.

David moved more than Moe did, rebounding with the force of the shove. He was afraid in that moment, afraid that Moe would kill or cripple the boy on the ground, afraid that Moe would turn his fury on David. But he stepped over Brad and stood chest to chest with Moe. "Enough. For Christ's sake, Moe. That's enough."

Moe, to his relief, looked indignant rather than enraged. "Do you mind? I'm in the middle of something here."

Brad rolled over and brought his knees up. He curled his arms protectively around his head and stared at David and Moe with wide, frightened eyes.

"I think he gets the message," David said drily. "Come on. Let's go."

"We should put him in the fucking hospital." Heat was creeping back into Moe's voice. "It's the only way fuckers like him learn." He took a half-step, trying to circle around David. Brad cringed and tried to squirm back without lowering his arms and legs.

David put an arm out, blocking Moe. His thin pale arm seemed like a poor barrier, but Moe stopped. "I'm hungry, Moe. I don't want to spend my lunch hour in the principal's office." He glanced at Brad. "Or a police station."

There was a bad moment when he thought Moe would push past him and finish what he'd started. The boy's shoulders dropped, though, the tension leaving him. He gave David a hard look. "They better be good."

"Huh?"

"The 'yo mama' jokes."

David gave a startled laugh, then stepped out of the way. He picked up his lunch, leaving the broken glass on the steps, and shook off a few drops of orange juice. "Or what? You'll get her to sit on me?"

Moe snickered, stepping over Brad, who tried to burrow into the sidewalk. Moe retrieved his own lunch, then looked around. "So much for eating outside."

They walked back up the steps. Brad's friends hadn't moved during the whole altercation. Now they pressed themselves back against the railings as the two boys went past. Moe gave them a sneering glance before re-entering the school.

Holy shit. Did that really just happen? The tranquility of the corridor was surreal after the violence of a moment before. David, jumpy and wired with leftover adrenalin, gave the boy beside him an uneasy glance. *What would he have done if I hadn't stopped him?*

"I hate fuckers like that." There was a strange tone to Moe's voice, a mix of sadness and resentment. "They used to call me Ahab the A-rab." He made an aggrieved face. "I'm Persian, for fuck's sake."

David, with no idea what the difference was, didn't comment. He thought of the moments before the fight, coming through the doors with Moe on his right, seeing Brad on his left. *Nobody did anything to Moe. He saw what Brad did, and he flipped.*

"There's only one way to make them stop," Moe said. "You have to fuck them up."

Brad was clearly a stand-in for whoever had bullied Moe in the past. It had nothing, really, to do with David. Nevertheless, he said, "Thanks."

Moe waved that away. "I should be the one thanking you. I don't need to get expelled again. I'm running out of schools to go to." He flashed a wry grin. "I don't think I'd fit in at Bishop Grandin. Besides, you helped me with the loop stuff. I owed you one."

They walked into the cafeteria and sat at an empty table. Moe said, "You really helped, too. I was going to skip tomorrow. Maybe the rest of the week. I felt so stupid. But I get it now." He took a Tupperware container out of his lunch bag and pushed it across the table. "Enough chatter. Give me the jelly sandwich."

Seven

I can't remember what Persian food tastes like. The thought was laughably trivial, but it stuck with David as he walked. What he needed to remember was a phone number for Moe, an address, even a last name that he might be able to look up. But with so much gone from the fabric of his life, he yearned for the simplest things, the memories that gave texture to a life.

He came to a bridge and leaned on the railing, watching water flow past below. *I used to stop here every day.* When he pursued the thought it retreated, so he focussed on the water and let his mind drift. *I crossed this bridge on my way to the CTrain. That means I lived near here.*

Turning, he resumed walking, scanning the condos and apartment buildings that lined the street. None of it looked even vaguely familiar, and he blew out a frustrated sigh.

I walked here with her. The thought crept up on him after a block or so spent staring at his feet. *Sometimes she held my hand. Other times she'd skip ahead, do a twirl, lag behind because a squirrel or a chickadee caught her*

*eye. Then she'd run up behind me, crash into me, almost
bowl me over. Laugh at me if I got annoyed.*

"Who are you?" he whispered to the girl from his
dream. "How do I find you?"

And where have you been? He didn't voice the
thought, even in a whisper. *Why did you let me get
locked away in an institution? Did you even visit?*

Maybe she did, said the cold voice in his mind. *Would
you even remember?*

Frustration washed over him, hot and bitter. Then
vanished when a voice said, "Holy shit! That's him!"

David looked up. Three young men were getting out
of a parked car just a few paces ahead of him. A blond
man, the top of his head coming no higher than David's
chin, slapped the arm of the man beside him. "Look!" He
pointed at David. "It's that guy from the news!"

Keep walking. It was the only strategy he could think
of. *Fake your way through.* He puckered his forehead,
just like he'd practiced in the nurse's bathroom. *I'm
puzzled and a bit bored. Totally not worried in the
slightest.*

"Dude!" The short man stepped into David's path,
grinning like he was sharing a joke. "Dude, you look just
like that guy!" He turned to the man beside him. "What
was his name?"

David stepped around him, heart thumping.

"David Alan Parkinson!"

David froze.

"Buddy!" There was nothing threatening in the man's manner as he put a hand on David's arm. He just looked excited. "Check this out. You look just like him!"

He produced a cell phone, and the others gathered around. One man peered over the blond man's shoulder. The third man was tall enough to stand behind and look over the top of the blond man's head.

David, sweat springing out across his body, looked at the phone. The muscles in his legs were as rigid as concrete posts. He couldn't have run if he'd tried. And he suddenly, desperately wanted to know what the man was going to show him.

"Just a sec." The man tapped and swiped. "There."

David's face filled the phone's tiny screen.

"Not him." The man who spoke was almost a head taller than David. He had to be a foot and a half taller than his friend. He squinted down at David, tilted his head, then looked at the phone. "The eyes are totally different."

"It's close, though." The short man looked from the phone to David and back. "You could totally be his older brother."

What do they mean? That's exactly what I look like. David fought an urge to put a hand on the man's shoulder as the world tilted around him. Static filled his ears. Only a desperate need to look calm kept him from clutching the sides of his head.

The face staring out from the phone's screen was him, all right. He recognized it. He could even remember when it was taken. *I was in a park. The photographer was ....*

The memory vanished, and he didn't pursue it, turning his thoughts instead to the mirror in his grungy room in Red Deer. His reflection had never seemed quite right, and now he understood why.

"He's ...." The effort of choosing words broke the panicky looping spiral of David's thoughts, and the buzzing in his ears faded. David put a hand to his own face. "He's a bit chubbier in the cheeks."

That was putting it kindly. David's face now was gaunt, his short hair salted with grey. The man in the photo, brown hair curling onto his shoulders, had a soft, relaxed, carefree look. *He's so young! My God. How long was I away?*

"I guess he's not quite your double," the short man said, deflating. He held the phone up by David's face for a side-by-side comparison. "He's close, though."

"Who is he?" David said, marvelling at the calm sound of his own voice.

The short man's energy returned. "He killed someone!" He swiped at the phone with a stubby finger. The others moved off, losing interest. The tall man opened the trunk of the car.

Another face filled the phone screen. A face David recognized instantly. The static came back, drowning out the man's next words.

Ashley Thomson—Victim, was the caption under the picture. The next photo was David and Ashley together in someone's back yard, his arm around her shoulders.

The David in the photo looked self-consciously at the camera. Ashley had her eyes fixed on him, her expression so tender it broke his heart.

The man swiped, and the picture changed to a young man. He wore a baseball cap, and his upper lip curled in a sneer. The caption said, *Cameron Bagwell—Victim.*

"... I mean, what the hell, am I right? He should have been in prison."

David tore his gaze from the phone. "Um, what?"

The short man narrowed his eyes. "He broke out of some loony bin," he said. "Must be nice. Kill two people, plead insanity, you don't even have to go to prison. Am I right?"

"When?" David shook his head, trying to clear it. "When did it happen?"

"Today, I think. Maybe last night? It was on the evening news." The trunk slammed, and the man looked toward his companions. "I—"

"I mean the murders," David blurted. *He's getting bored. Let him go. Give him a chance to forget all about you.* He had to know, though. "When did the murders happen?"

The man shrugged. "I don't know. Like, five years ago? Listen, I gotta go." He turned, then paused, lifting the phone. "Hey, can I do a selfie with you? I wanna show—"

"No." David brushed past him and hurried away.

Five years. I lost five years. He shuddered. *At least I'm not an old man.* He thought of his reflection. *I look like I've aged a decade at least.*

He did his best to cling to that thought, but it crumbled away, leaving him with no more distractions. The one thought he wanted most to avoid seeped in, insidious as a winter chill.

She's dead. She's been dead for five years. I only just started to remember her, and I'll never see her again.

Eight

Ashley.

Her ghost swirled around him, one moment so sharp and alive that his eyes filled with tears, the next as wispy and abstract as if he were remembering someone else's stories, as if she were someone he'd heard about but never met. He struggled to bring her into focus, until the only part that felt real was the memory of his dream.

At last he gave up, feeling hollowed out and exhausted and terribly alone. His feet hurt, but he kept walking because he couldn't just stop in the middle of the sidewalk.

He touched his face, exploring his features with his fingers, trying to feel the changes. He traced the edges of his ears. *They stick out. I always wore my hair long because my ears looked so stupid.*

Now he had the haircut of a military recruit. He touched his hairline, then reached up and put his palm flat on the top of his head. His hand was too small, his fingers too short, for the memory that teased him. *Grandpa did that. He ruffled my hair. I must have been so small.*

He wanted to cling to that moment, but it came with a long, bitter tail. He let it fade.

Moe would laugh if he could see me now. The specifics eluded him, but he was sure he and Moe had become friends, sticking together even when high school ended. *So how come he never came to see me in Red Deer?*

Because visiting people in institutions is awful. David shivered. *Remember that time you went to see Matt?*

David touched his hair one more time, but this time it was Matthew in his memory, ruffling David's hair with the good-natured contempt of an older brother as he walked past. He lived on his own, eking out a living delivering pizzas. It was his first dinner at home since moving out. He took the chair beside David at the dinner table, speared a pork chop, and dropped it on his plate.

"Take another one. You're so thin!" Mom had three months' worth of pent-up fussing to get through, and she wasn't holding anything back. "David, pass him the mashed potatoes."

"I have some potatoes."

"You hardly took any. Have you been eating?" She didn't wait for an answer. "Are you getting enough sleep? I don't know how you can stand it, living with so many people in such a tiny house. Is it noisy?"

"Well, nobody yells." Matthew flicked a glance at Dad. "That helps. And if someone stays up 'til two in the morning to watch a movie, so what? I mean, what's the point in being an adult if you can't chill out and do what you want sometimes?"

"Sounds nice." The instant the words were out of David's mouth he knew he'd blundered. *Stupid! When will you learn? Never talk at home.*

Dad's head swivelled around. His eyes were dark and malevolent, but his mouth curved up in a parody of friendliness. "Are you not satisfied with the way things are run around here, David?"

"Sorry." David fixed his gaze on his plate. "Nothing. Sorry."

In his peripheral vision Dad leaned forward to stare down the table at him. "I said, are you unsatisfied? Do you have any complaints?" And after a moment of squirming silence, "Answer me!"

David, frightened and humiliated, choked the words out, one at a time. "No ... sorry ... I didn't mean—"

"David doesn't like the way we run things." Dad looked at the rest of the embarrassed family, wearing a mocking smile though his fists were clenched, the muscles in his forearms rigid. "Never mind that I told him to mow the lawn four days ago and he still hasn't done it. He thinks we have too many rules!"

"Oh, for fuck's sake."

The F-bomb was enough to make the whole family gape at Matthew as he stood. "Sorry, Mom." He gestured at his plate. "I had a few bites. It was good." He turned and headed for the front door.

"Sit down!"

"Sure, Dad." Matthew didn't stop. "Whatever you say." He walked out.

There was a long moment of silence. Mom stared at the door, her face devastated. Dad looked stricken, but it didn't take long for fury to reassert itself. There was never any question what his target would be.

"You." He stabbed a thick forefinger at David, his voice rising with every word. "We have our first real family dinner in a month, and you have to ruin it."

David, who knew better than to argue, kept his eyes on his plate and his mouth shut. Dad's rant went on for forty-five minutes. Food got cold on their plates, the gravy congealed, as the three of them sat in miserable silence and waited for it to end. Dad shouted and thrashed the air with his arms, and when he finished, he curtly ordered everyone to finish their suppers. So they spooned down balls of cold mashed potatoes with cubes of gravy on top until Mom and Emily could safely dart out of the room.

David went outside and cut the lawn, front and back, in the dark. Then he went to bed, where he lay in the dark, sick with rage and humiliation, wishing his father dead.

He was on the verge of sleep when the ringing of a telephone roused him. He lay still and listened while Dad's muffled voice spoke, paused, then spoke again, louder. Mom gave a low cry, and David stared at the ceiling, wondering what was going on.

He heard his parents dressing and wondered if he should dress too. Surely in a moment his bedroom door would open and they would tell him what was happening.

Instead, a honk from outside made them scamper across the house and out the front door. David got up then, in time to see a taxi pull away from the curb. He wandered downstairs, baffled.

"What is it?"

He turned to see Emily on the stairs. "I don't know."

They sat up for a couple of hours, sure something was dreadfully wrong but with no idea what to do. Dad didn't believe in cell phones, which meant Mom didn't have one either. Emily texted Matthew. She got no response.

"Normal people don't do this."

David looked at Emily and raised his eyebrows.

"Leave in the middle of the night," she said. "Not even tell us where they're going."

He shrugged. To Dad it would make perfect sense. Waking his kids up to keep them informed would send the wrong message. He was trying to teach them proper humility, after all. Mom wouldn't like it, but she would never contradict him.

There was no point in talking about it to Emily. The rules were different for her. He went back to bed, not because he thought he could sleep, but because Dad would be furious if he came home and found them up.

Early the next morning he answered the doorbell to find Aunt Sheila, Mom's sister, on the doorstep. Sheila, almost as timid as Mom, was deathly afraid of David's father. She didn't ever come to visit. The sight of her at the front door scared David more than the long night's vigil had done.

She came in without being asked. When Emily appeared, Sheila said, "Matthew's been in a car accident. A bad one."

David stared at her, trying to make his voice work. *Is Matthew dead?* He couldn't make himself speak the words out loud.

"He's badly hurt," Sheila said. She clasped her hands, squeezing so tight her fingers turned white.

Emily said, "Will he ...."

"I don't know."

She packed up some things for David's parents. Then she drove David and Emily to the hospital.

Only Matthew's head, encased in bandages, and one arm, hung with tubes, were visible. A sheet covered the rest. Dad stood by the window, staring at the floor. He didn't look up when the rest of the family came in.

Mom, of course, was more emotional. She jumped up from her chair with a sob, hugging David and Emily, then Sheila. The two women clung to each other and wept loudly, making David hope irreverently that Matt wouldn't have a long convalescence. *If he dies they'll be insufferable.*

If he dies. The fear he'd been suppressing closed in, squeezing him from throat to groin like a terrible fist. He fought to breathe. Only the fact that his stomach was empty kept him from vomiting.

He looked at his brother, trying to burn every detail into his brain as the room lapsed into silence. Not much of Matt actually showed. He watched Matt's eyelids and a little patch of forehead exposed between the oxygen mask and the bandages around his head. David tried to memorize the image, thinking with a disbelieving horror that that bit of skin might be sealed in a box a week from now, lowered into the earth to slowly rot.

The vigil stretched out until he couldn't stand it any longer. He backed quietly out of the room and wandered down the hospital corridor.

Nurses smiled at him sympathetically. An ancient and decrepit woman went past in a wheelchair, surrounded by a gaggle of solicitous relatives. Someone in the distance began an indignant wailing.

At the end of the corridor he found a nurses' station and a wall with several windows. He crossed to the windows and gazed outside. *It looks like it's going to rain.*

"Hello, David."

Nine years of his life fell away in the time it took him to turn his head. He threw his arms around his grandfather, conscious for the first time of the need to be gentle. He held on for a long time.

At last they stepped apart and looked at each other for the first time since David's eighth birthday. Grandpa's shoulders were a little more stooped than David remembered. He was shorter than David, which seemed impossible.

They found a lounge and sat on ersatz leather couches. Grandpa said, "I was starting to think you forgot about me." He smiled as he said it.

David smiled back. "Why would you ever think that?"

The old man rummaged in a pocket, found a tissue, wiped his eyes, and blew his nose. "Well, I haven't heard from you since I moved."

David said, "You moved?"

For the first time Grandpa's smile faltered. "They didn't tell you?"

David shook his head.

Grandpa's voice was low and hoarse now. "It happened about three and a half years ago. Your grandmother had a stroke. She's in a nursing home here in the city. I wanted to be able to visit her more easily. And I'm getting too old to farm." He sighed. "So I got a place close to the nursing home. I've been enjoying my retirement ever since."

His voice rang a bit hollow on that last sentence.

David stared at him, unable to take it in.

Grandpa's gaze shifted to the left. A guarded look crossed his face, and David turned, knowing what he would see.

Dad walked toward them, his face stiff and blank. David bounced to his feet, full of a sudden fury that burned so bright he forgot to be scared. He stepped close and snarled, "Why didn't you tell me?"

For the briefest moment Dad's face went slack. There might have been shame in his eyes. Maybe even regret. Then the muscles in his face tightened, his habitual rage returning.

David stood nose to nose with him, marvelling at the novelty of not being afraid. He thought of all the things he might say. He thought about simply planting a fist in the man's face.

Or I could go punch that wall over there. Or shout at it. It would do as much good.

Dad opened his mouth, and David spun on his heel and strode away.

He pushed through a set of double doors, stomped down a flight of stairs, and followed an exit sign. He wanted to slam a door or two, but the next set of doors slid open as he approached. He stalked outside. When the first raindrops hit him he retreated to an overhang, where he watched the rain increase until it was a downpour.

A hand landed on his shoulder. David didn't turn, but his grandfather spoke anyway.

"Are you all right?"

"I don't know."

The hand squeezed his shoulder. Grandpa moved up to stand beside him. "You're all right."

David said, "I can't live with that—" He paused, unwilling to swear in front of his grandfather. "That jerk anymore."

Grandpa's voice was surprisingly hard. "Yes, you can."

David looked at him, startled.

"You're seventeen. In a short time you'll be an adult. You'll be free. Your father won't matter. You won't need him. Unless you screw your life up right now."

David, choking on a knot of frustrated anger, didn't answer.

"Besides, your family is going through a terrible time. Your mother and your sister are decent people. They don't need you running away from home on top of everything else. They need you here."

David nodded miserably. "Well, will I at least be able to see you in the meantime?"

A bleak look crossed Grandpa's face. "No."

"What?"

Grandpa said, "He's bad enough now. If you try to stay in touch with me, he'll get worse. I've had it with that boy. He can go shit in a boot."

For the first time David caught a glimpse of the hard, sarcastic man his father had learned to hate.

Grandpa grinned at the expression on his face. "It's all right, David. I've waited this long to get to know you again, and I can wait a little longer." He turned, making a "come along" gesture. "Let's go see Matthew."

David didn't move.

"David? What is it?"

"I can't stand it." The words filled him with shame, but they tumbled out, impossible to stop. "Standing around his bed. Waiting for him to die."

"Oh." Grandpa startled him by smiling. "I forgot the whole reason I came looking for you."

David stared at him, afraid to ask.

"Matthew came out of his coma. He's awake. It looks like he's going to be all right."

Nine

David shivered, shoving his hands into the pockets of his stolen jacket. Small apartment buildings surrounded him, none of them familiar. *I need to go back to the bridge. Figure out where I used to live. I don't need memories of high school. I need to remember what came later.*

I need to remember Ashley.

He turned around, realized he'd been walking blindly, and stopped. *How am I supposed to remember what happened five years ago when I don't remember the last half hour?* He turned in a circle, trying to get his bearings.

And stopped, staring at an apartment building. He recognized it. What he really recognized was the sign in front, proudly identifying the property as the Cambridge Arms. The building was a shabby brick rectangle completely undeserving of its pretentious name.

We would make fun of it, every time we went past. He approached the building, letting wisps of memory trickle into his brain. *We would turn at the corner with the giant tree. The one with the trailing branches.* The tree was always carefully pruned, but whoever did the pruning had to be five feet tall at the most. He remembered branches like delicate fingers brushing his hair, tickling his face as he walked underneath. *We made hobbit jokes. Bag End Landscaping. Best yard care company in the Shire.*

The tree was gone, but he found a stump, an oval of wood as wide as a dinner table cut flush with the surrounding lawn.

Where were we going? He shrugged to himself as he turned the corner. *I guess I'll find out when I get there.*

His stomach rumbled. Some nausea remained, but it seemed his appetite was returning. Only when he started salivating did he notice the smell, the irresistible aroma of deep fryer grease. He walked faster, rounding the next corner.

And stopped short.

A diner stood across the street, warm golden light spilling through the windows. The lettering on the battered green awning had faded into illegibility, but he knew what it said.

Pat's Place.

Pat's was the only restaurant in the neighbourhood that was open all night. *I came here with Ashley. It must have been three in the morning. We joked about how bad the food was going to be, but it was amazing. After that we came here all the time.*

Which means I might be recognized. Still, he walked across the street and into the light, helpless as a moth.

The tinkle of a bell sounded as loud as a fire alarm when he pushed the door open. A waitress gave him a weary glance and called, "Sit anywhere you like."

David, frozen in the doorway, took a deep breath and made himself step inside. A couple of old men sat at a table near the back, ignoring him. There were no other customers.

He slid into a booth with a view of the street. *This was our regular table.*

The smell of the place was mundane, a blend of grease and French fries and chilli sauce with an undertone of plastic from the fake leather seats, but it triggered waves of memory. Ashley sitting across from him. Ashley sliding in beside him. Ashley eating with one hand, the other hand squeezing his thigh.

She should be here. He stared out the window, not wanting to see the emptiness of the booth.

The waitress appeared, reflected in the glass, hefting a pot. "Coffee?"

Burned fresh every day. That was Ashley's joke. Coffee was the only thing on the menu that was less than excellent. "No," he said, not turning his head.

She set a menu down and walked away, and he watched a streetlight come on as shadows darkened outside. People trickled back and forth on the sidewalk. No one came into the diner.

He was about to reach for the menu when one pedestrian froze. A heavyset man in a puffy jacket, a cowboy shirt stretched tight where his stomach bulged over his blue jeans, stood on the sidewalk, staring at the diner.

Staring at David.

Don't be stupid. He's probably trying to decide if he's hungry. David looked away, but kept the man in his peripheral vision.

The man didn't move.

"What'll it be, hon?"

David looked at the waitress, then looked outside.

The man was gone.

"I can't stay." He slid out of the booth, imagining police cars surrounding the diner. He paused at the door and peered outside.

No sign of the stranger.

David hurried outside, hoping he was overreacting but knowing he'd never be able to eat. He gave the brightly lit street a distrustful glance and strode instead to the corner of the building. *Ashley and I used to cut through the alley. It's nice and dark. And it leads straight to ... where?*

He rounded the corner, and almost collided with a looming figure standing in the shadows. It was the man in the puffy jacket. He was young, in his twenties, with heavy features and a sullen look that made David think of Brad, the bully from high school. The two of them stood nose to nose, both of them momentarily startled.

"It's you." His voice was gruff, tentative, but it became more certain with every word. "It's really you."

David shook his head. "No, I just look like him, that guy on the news, he—"

Thick arms shot out, smacking into David's chest and shoving him back. David's shoulders hit the wall of the diner. He bounced forward, straight into another shove.

The impact with the wall was harder this time, driving the air from his lungs. The back of his head hit the bricks, and pain filled his skull.

Hands closed on David's jacket. The man's face contorted, his teeth appearing, his eyes all but vanishing into deep folds of flesh. He yanked David away from the wall, then slammed him backward, into the bricks. David gave a wheezing groan, the only sound he could manage with empty lungs. Strong hands gripped the sides of his head, then pulled forward. *He's going to slam my head against the wall.*

David let his knees buckle as the man began to shove. His skull slid out of the man's grasp, and knuckles thumped against brick above him. Momentum drove the man forward, his stomach hitting David's face. The man swore and straightened, and David threw himself sideways. He scrambled across the parking lot on all fours, made it onto his feet, and ran.

Shoes slapped the pavement behind him, loud as thunderclaps, as the man pursued. Headlights glowed in the street, and David headed toward them, waving his arms. The sound of running footsteps filled him with terror. *I can't stop.* He fled to the opposite sidewalk.

Brakes squealed behind him. The impact was awful, a metallic thud mixed with something much worse, a fleshy sound like a baseball smacking into a glove. David staggered to a halt and turned.

A car sat in the middle of the street, engine running, the driver a vague outline behind the wheel. The fat man lay on his back, an arm and a leg under the car's front bumper. He didn't move, and David put a hand to his mouth, filled with a sickening blend of relief and horror.

The man rolled onto his stomach, put both palms on the pavement, and pushed himself up. His head swung from side to side, then froze when he saw David. He winced as he drew in his legs, but he got one foot planted and started to rise.

David ran.

A car door creaked open behind him. A woman said, "Are you all right? Wait! Where are you going?"

David shot a glance over his shoulder. The fat man was hobbling after him, limping badly but refusing to stop.

When David got to the next corner he looked back again. The man was still coming, moving slowly but picking up speed. The limp was already less pronounced.

David hurried around the corner, knowing he could make the next intersection and disappear before the man came back into view. But his footsteps slowed when he came to the alley. *We always went around back when we left Pat's place. We always took the alley.*

Where were we going?

His instincts told him to turn left, to get as far as he could from the maniac chasing him. After a moment of inner struggle he turned right, toward the diner. *He won't expect me to double back, will he?*

The gravel in the alley was noisier than he liked. He ran past a couple of apartment buildings, then slid into the shadow of a dumpster. A stack of pizza boxes gave off an aroma of pepperoni, and he pushed away a sudden memory of pizza-and-a-movie night in Ashley's apartment. He considered curling into a ball where the shadows were deepest. Instead, he peeked around the dumpster.

Long seconds passed. He heard the slap of footsteps growing louder. It went on and on, and he marvelled at noise one man was able to produce.

Finally the man appeared. He went down the middle of the street, moving in a painful half-walk, half-jog. His right leg seemed stiff, but the limp was mostly gone. His head didn't turn as he passed between the mouths of two alleys. He lurched along, mindless and implacable, like something out of a nightmare.

When David could no longer hear footsteps, he left the shadow of the dumpster. He passed behind the diner, wondering if the driver had called the police. *Is it a hit and run if it's the pedestrian who runs away? Will they care? Did she recognize me from the news?*

He thought not. She'd barely caught a glimpse of him, and her attention would be on the man she hit.

What about him? He definitely recognized me. Will he call the cops? David shivered, remembering the demented snarl on the man's face. *Or does he want to kill me himself?*

No sirens howled in the distance. He pushed the worry to the back of his mind, where it joined a thousand other neglected fears, and kept walking.

At the end of the block he darted across the street and into another alley, sure without knowing why that he was going the right way. The apartment buildings gave way to bungalows and duplexes. He frowned at the bulk of a garage. *That wasn't here before.*

There was nothing distinctive about the chest-high board fence across from the garage. Nevertheless he recognized it. The gate would brush against a set of wind chimes if you opened it, making a considerable racket. But the third board from the corner was loose. He and Ashley used to sneak into the garden and steal carrots. They weren't all that fond of raw carrots, and these carrots had bits of dirt still clinging to them. But *stolen* raw carrots had a special flavour all their own.

The alley curved, and things grew more familiar with every step. He passed board fences, chain link fences, a hedge. *I'm almost there.*

Almost where?

I don't know.

He reached a low picket fence and looked into an ordinary back yard. A small lawn, a bit of garden, a bird bath. A bungalow with pale green siding. *I'm here. Wherever* here *is.*

Dark windows stared down on a shadowed yard. Guided by a vague whisper of instinct, David reached forward and unlatched the gate.

A little table and a pair of metal chairs stood just past the spreading branches of a small tree. He remembered sitting there on sunny afternoons, watching birds squabbling in—yes, there by the back door, a bird feeder.

David crossed to the table and sat in one of the chairs. *This was her house. Ashley lived here. No, that can't be right. She had an apartment.* Images flickered through his mind, hitting a buzzer, climbing stairs, cuddling on the couch in her tiny living room.

She brought me here. I was so nervous. I tried to talk her out of it, but she called me a big chicken. There was someone she wanted me to meet. Who was it?

The back door opened and a man came out. He was in late middle age, with broad shoulders and a hint of a paunch. He had the blunt, rugged features of a Hollywood lumberjack. He wore a plaid shirt and blue jeans, which heightened the illusion, but David knew he was a petroleum geologist.

He stood a moment on the back step, looking at David. He had a kind face, lined by equal measures of laughter and sorrow. David remembered his eyes being warm and blue. He remembered fewer wrinkles, and not so much white in the man's ginger hair. The family resemblance wasn't obvious at first, but it was there in the set of his mouth and the shape of his eyes.

The man walked slowly across the yard and sat down on the other chair. He said, "Hello, David."

"Hello, Mr. Thomson."

Ten

David met Ashley by crashing into her. It was a cold November day and he was in a hurry to get home while he still had some feeling in his hands. Some oaf bumped him going the other way, and David turned his head, glaring at the offender. "Why don't you watch where you're—"

She must have seen him coming and braced herself, because she kept her footing as he collided with her. He landed sprawling, staring at a pair of leggings decorated with comic book sound effects. His gaze went from her right shin ('POW!') to her left knee ('BAM!'), across an expanse of fuzzy blue jacket, and reached her face.

She folded her arms, looked down at him, and arched an eyebrow. In that instant David forgot all about being annoyed, or cold, or anything else. He started to speak, discovered his mind was blank, and sat there with his mouth open.

"It's okay." Her cheeks dimpled. "Guys fall for me all the time."

Only hours later, when he replayed the scene in his mind, did he realize she'd made a joke. Because he had fallen for her, instantaneously, completely, and permanently.

He got up, flustered and stammering, aware that he'd met the girl he'd been waiting for all his life and blown it in the space of a single heartbeat. The creases in her cheeks deepened with every clumsy word of his apology. Finally she lifted a gloved hand and put a finger against his lips.

"Hush. Your blandishments don't impress me. Talk is cheap. Hot chocolate, however, is expensive."

David scrabbled through his suddenly feverish brain, searching for a response that was suave, or charming, or at least coherent. What he came up with was, "Huh?"

"Smooth talker," she said, and stepped up beside him. "I like that." She hooked a hand through his elbow. "You're going to buy me a hot chocolate. It's the least you can do."

He gaped at her. She met his gaze, and did the eyebrow-lifting thing again. Her air of utter self-assurance left him hopelessly flustered—until she spoiled it by biting her lower lip, just for a moment. She changed from a dazzling, unearthly goddess to a girl, worried how a boy would react to her, and David, with an inward sigh of relief, finally knew how to respond.

He closed his mouth and gave her a solemn nod, as if this conversation were perfectly ordinary and not the most surreal thing to happen to him in months. "I was just thinking the same thing."

Her grin, cool and aloof, was replaced for just an instant by a genuine smile, a blend of delight and relief that warmed him all the way to his toes. It was a good thing she had a hand on his arm because it was the only thing keeping his feet on the sidewalk as she walked him down the street.

He met her father two weeks later. David wore a crisp white shirt he had laboured over with an iron. Then he fidgeted and sweated until the shirt looked slept in by the time they reached the house.

Mr. Thomson opened the door and sized David up in one glance. He fixed the nervous young man with a cold glare and snapped, "So, you're the boy who's going out with my daughter?"

"Um, yes, Sir."

Ashley, by this time, was rolling her eyes and sighing out loud. Her father drew his brows together and leaned closer to David. "Are you trying to be funny, young man?"

"What?" *Don't look terrified. Ashley is watching.* "No! No, Sir, um, Mr. Thomson."

"Then what are you doing on my doorstep with your fly undone?"

David looked down, horrified. His zipper was done up.

Mr. Thomson laughed, clapping him on the shoulder. "I'm sorry, David. I couldn't resist. Come in, boy, come in."

"Uh ... thank you, Sir."

"Oh, for pity's sake, call me Aaron. Come in. Hi, sweetie."

Ashley punched her father lightly on the arm before letting him kiss her cheek.

He served them fried chicken for supper, regaling them with embarrassing tales from Ashley's early childhood and, to be fair, an equal number of embarrassing stories from his own chequered youth. He quickly put David at ease.

After that David and Ashley dined at his house about once a week. Aaron was a source of infinite warmth, good humour, and offbeat wisdom. He laced his conversation with such aphorisms as, "An ounce of prevention is worth a pound of gauze bandages," and "If you argue with nay-sayers, you'll just make yourself hoarse." To David he became a role model and surrogate father.

Now Aaron leaned an elbow on the little table and stared soberly at David. "Well?" he said at last. "Want to tell me about it?"

David took a deep breath. "I .... Aaron, I don't remember what happened. That night. I don't .... Aaron, people say I killed Ashley."

Aaron snorted. "Nonsense. I think I know you better than that."

"But what if—"

"I know Ashley, too."

David blinked at the non sequitur. "What?"

"The police theory," Aaron said, his voice turning hard and brittle, "is that she cheated on you with her ex-boyfriend." He grimaced. "Supposedly you walked in on them, snapped, and killed them both." His hand swiped at the air, as if physically tossing such nonsense aside.

"Then you apparently stabbed yourself in the stomach before having a full-blown nervous breakdown. You were the only witness, and you weren't talking. So they made up a cockamamie theory and decided to run with it. Cops have a saying. It's always the nearest and dearest. The husband, the wife, the boyfriend. They figured it had to be you."

David looked down and found his hand rubbing unconsciously at the scar on his stomach. "So ... what happened, then?"

"The cops were almost right." The disgust on Aaron's face changed to sour anger. "They got the wrong boyfriend, that's all. It was Cameron Bagwell. I never liked that boy. And when Ashley left him, he went unbalanced. I saw how she was with him. She was unhappy every day. And I saw how she was with you. It was like the sun came up for her. The only dark spot was the way that little prick kept showing up to bother her every few months."

Aaron's eyebrows came together, his expression so fierce that David drew back. "Cameron finally figured out it was over. He'd never get her back. He couldn't take it. So he broke into her apartment and he raped her."

Aaron's eyes closed briefly. He took a deep breath, opened his eyes, and stared bleakly at David. When he spoke, his voice was haggard and old.

"He raped her and he killed her, and then you came in. The two of you fought. He stabbed you, but you got the scissors away from him. And you did what you had to do.

"And, David, the only comfort I've had over the years since then is knowing that you avenged my Ashley for me." He shifted, looking past David's head, staring into the darkness. "You're a gentle boy. Having to kill someone, even a murderous piece of shit like Cameron Bagwell .... Well, it broke you. But I want you to know. You did the right thing."

Silence fell over the dark back yard. David focussed on his breathing, trying not to picture the horrors Aaron had described. *Dear God, he killed her with a pair of scissors?*

"You'll have to tell me how you broke out of Lougheed."

David looked at Aaron, who wore a hint of a smile. "Law ...?"

"The Lougheed Institute," Aaron said. "That's where they put you. I kept hoping you'd recover. Tell your side of it. Get them to let you out." His eyes crinkled in amusement. "I always knew one day I'd turn on the news and see your face. I never thought it would be for a breakout."

The enormity of it all sank in, and David slumped in his seat. "What's going to happen to me now?"

Aaron shrugged. "Well, you never had a trial. I guess you'll finally get your day in court." He stood. "Never mind that for now. You've had one hell of a day. Come on." He gestured. "You can sleep here tonight. In the morning I'll find you a lawyer. We'll get this sorted out."

David stood as well. "The police are after me, aren't they? Maybe I shouldn't stay here."

"Bull." Aaron took his arm. "You're staying, and that's final." He tugged David toward the house. "We'll get you a good lawyer, and then we'll deal with the cops. But that's a problem for tomorrow. Come on. Let's go inside."

Taking the first step toward the house felt like stepping off a cliff. There was a moment of terror that faded by the second step, but he still felt like he was falling. By the third step he knew the feeling wasn't free-fall. Not weightlessness. It was weight reduction. The boulder on his shoulders, terror and confusion and above all a dreadful isolation, was gone. He felt as light as thistle down.

Aaron went first into the dark house. He turned on a light over the stove, bathing the kitchen in a soft warm glow. When he turned back to David his eyes widened. "Sit down! You look like you're about to collapse."

Aaron gestured at a chair, and David plopped himself down. He felt as if he'd been running laps, pushing himself until there was nothing left. He put an elbow on the kitchen table and rested his chin on his palm, the only way he could keep his head up.

"I'll get some blankets. You sit tight." Aaron left the kitchen. David traced out the familiar nicks in the tabletop with his fingertip. *He better hurry with the blankets. I'm going to fall asleep right here.*

Floorboards creaked behind him, and David turned in his chair. And the world lurched around him.

Ashley stood in the kitchen doorway.

Eleven

She caught him before he fell out of the chair. With a hard shove she got him back upright, then clung to his arm to keep him from toppling the other way. Her face was inches away from his, her features lifted straight from his anguished memory. But she had a tiny crooked scar by her right eyebrow. He remembered that scar.

David took a deep breath and steadied himself. "Hi, Kim."

She stared at him without recognition. Then her eyes widened, and she screamed.

Kim didn't always look like her older sister. When David met her, she was a gangly sixteen-year-old who blushed and bolted from the room every time he came over.

That first dinner she stared at her plate through the entire meal, never saying a word. Over the following months she relaxed somewhat, but was never exactly bubbly. Sometimes in the late evenings Aaron would go to bed and the three young people would sit up watching movies. Then David would glance over to find Kim gazing at him surreptitiously. She would turn red and look away, never speaking.

Ashley thought her sister's obvious crush was hilarious, and teased her mercilessly. David was flattered and sympathetic. He tried to be nice to her, though if he paid her too much attention she left the room.

Now she stood before him in a frayed bathrobe and flannel nightgown. Her hair, shorter that Ashley's had been, was scattered in an untidy halo around her face. Her small red lips were pursed, the freckles on her nose standing out as her face went pale. Her amber eyes, so much like Ashley's, were wide and frightened.

For a long moment they stared at each other, both of them shaking. Then Aaron stepped into the doorway and took her shoulders in his hands. She spun around and clung to him, and they moved out of David's sight.

For five long minutes he sat alone in the kitchen, trying to find the strength to leave. At last Aaron returned. "Would you like a little coffee?"

David shook his head.

"Then I won't make any." Aaron gave him a small, strained grin. "I'll have enough trouble getting any sleep tonight as it is." He leaned forward, patting David on the shoulder. "It's all right, son. I talked to Kim and got her calmed down. She's okay. You just caught her by surprise."

David made himself smile.

"Anyway, come on."

The living room boasted a small fireplace in one corner. Aaron stirred the remains of a fire, added bits of kindling, and coaxed it back to life.

When the couch was fitted with sheets and blankets, Aaron clapped him on the shoulder once more and headed off to bed. David sat for a while on the edge of the couch. He was exhausted, but he felt no real desire to sleep. His head ached, but the pain felt distant, easy to ignore.

He crossed to the fireplace and squatted, fed in sticks, and watched the flames stretch out questing fingers. He took the poker, prodded the burning wood, then let his eyes lose focus as he watched the fire.

He didn't know how much time had passed when he heard a light step behind him.

Kim stood in the entrance to the living room. She wore only the flannel nightgown, and the curves of her body were painfully familiar. Her eyes were bleak and hard, her face determined.

She held a pistol in her hand, levelled at him.

David sighed. *I never really appreciated the Lougheed Institute. All that peace and quiet.*

"This is Dad's gun. He bought it after Ashley was killed. After you killed her." Her voice was a cold whisper. "You killed her."

She walked into the room and stopped a couple of feet away from him. The barrel of the pistol wavered but never quite strayed from his chest.

"Before I shoot you, David, there's one thing you can do you for me. You can satisfy my curiosity."

He opened his mouth, but no words came out.

"How could you do it? How could you stab my sister?" Her face twisted. "With *scissors*!"

They stared at each other, the gun wobbling between them. "I couldn't," he said. "I couldn't hurt her. Not ever."

"Bastard." She cocked the pistol, the sound so loud in the quiet room that for a moment David thought she'd shot him. "You son of a bitch. Goodbye."

The gun stopped wavering. He looked at the muzzle, the trigger, her finger. The skin on her knuckle whitened.

"What if it wasn't me?"

The question caught her by surprise. Her eyebrows rose, her gaze went to his face—and in one quick motion he plucked the gun from her hand.

It was a compact revolver, so small it looked like a toy. He pointed it carefully into the fireplace and eased the hammer down.

Kim gaped at him. She looked at the gun, then at the poker he still held in his other hand.

"Oh, for God's sake." He put the poker back in its rack. "I'm not going to hurt you." He pushed the gun into her hand. She stared at him, eyes wide in a pale, bloodless face.

He turned and closed the mesh curtain in front of the fire, then stepped around her and sat on the couch. *I didn't do it.* There was no point in saying the words, so he kept silent as he pulled off his shoes and socks. When he looked up again, he was alone.

He started to unbutton his jeans. Paused. Kim would call the police, or the fat man from the diner would, or the cops would track him down on their own. He would be awakened by the sound of police bursting in the front door. He no longer cared. *Still, I'd rather be arrested wearing pants.*

The couch was long enough that he could stretch out. A lumpy cushion pressed into the bruises on his back, so he shifted onto his side. He drew Aaron's blankets up to his chin, yawned, and let the world fade away.

A floorboard creaked. Feet rustled on carpet. Then silence.

If she's going to shoot me, I better make sure she aims for the head. David opened his eyes.

Kim stood over him. Her hands were empty. She gazed at him, sad and silent. Then she knelt and her hand touched his shoulder. She whispered, "I'm sorry. I really thought you did it." Her lips brushed his cheek, and she stood and scampered away.

David watched her go, one hand touching his cheek. *The Thomson sisters have quite a knack for keeping me off balance.*

The lumps in the couch had mysteriously vanished. He was warm and comfortable, but he knew he had to leave. *Aaron and Kim have suffered enough. I can't bring trouble to their door. I'll walk back to the diner and ask that waitress to call the police.*

He was trying to decide whether to wake Aaron up or just slip out when he fell asleep.

When Ashley slid into the booth across from him, he knew he was dreaming. He reached across the table, took her hands, and clung to them, drinking in every detail of her face. "Oh, Ashley. It's good to see you."

She gave him a mocking grin, but he could see she was pleased.

"I've missed you," he said. "I've missed you so much."

"Well, you should have saved me, then." She still wore her mocking grin. "I'm very disappointed, David. You were supposed to protect me." She tugged her hands free.

He was searching for a reply when she glanced out the window. "Oh, hell. Here we go again."

Two men stood in the parking lot. One was fat, the other thin, but their long, sharp-nosed faces were similar enough to mark them as brothers. The Bagwell brothers. The fat one, Nathan, wore a cowboy shirt. He was younger than David remembered, his hair shorter. He looked right at David but didn't react.

The thin man, Cameron, was smoothing his clothes, his gaze fixed on Ashley through the window. He didn't seem to realize she could see him as easily as he could see her. He took out a comb, touched up his hair, and checked his reflection on the back of his phone.

Nathan punched him on the shoulder, apparently a gesture of encouragement. Cameron spent a moment fidgeting, then headed for the entrance.

Ashley pointed her thumb at Nathan. "His brother's a little creepy."

Creepy? He's a maniac. David forgot Nathan as Cameron entered the diner, visibly gathered himself, then marched toward them. He stopped beside the booth, staring at Ashley, ignoring David. Ashley kept her gaze fixed on David, her posture rigid, her face cold and blank.

David leaned forward, examining this man who had somehow won Ashley's heart before David came along. He wasn't actually thin, without Nathan beside him for contrast. Cameron had an athletic build. He was even kind of good-looking, in an unconvincing way. He had the chiselled jaw of a TV actor, like the football player who almost gets the girl before she realizes she's in love with the sensitive nerd.

He spoiled the effect when he opened his mouth.

"I'm sorry I smashed your stuff." Cameron spread his hands in a helpless, frustrated gesture. "I was just so mad. I shouldn't of done it. I won't do it again."

Ashley didn't speak, didn't move. She hardly breathed.

Cameron droned on for several minutes, promising to change, offering to replace everything he'd destroyed in a furious tantrum, apologizing for all the names he'd called her, all the vicious emails and texts. He swore he loved her and begged her to give him another chance.

Ashley didn't react, except for an eyeroll only David could see.

Cameron's voice trailed off, and at last he said, "Well? Can we try again?"

Ashley shook her head, a small, quick motion that drained the life from Cameron's face, leaving his features slack and ill. His fists clenched, and David tensed.

"Bitch." Cameron spun and stalked out of the diner. Nathan trotted over, following him out of the parking lot like a vast puppy.

"Never date someone in your own neighborhood," Ashley said, her flippant tone not quite hiding an underlying tension. "You keep running into them." She cocked an eyebrow at David. "That's what I like about you. It takes, like, an hour to walk to your place."

He gave her a weak grin. "Well, I'm glad you like something about me."

She looked him up and down like she was inspecting something in a dollar store and thinking about putting it back on the shelf. "You're okay in bed, too." She smirked.

He gave her his best hurt look, which made her snicker. Then she reached across the table and took his hand. "I'm sorry we don't have much time together. Don't let him kill you, okay, babe?" Her smile became strained, her face going pale. "Getting killed sucks."

"Ashley!" Her hand was cold in his, her face bone white, as if all the blood had drained from her body. "Ashley, no."

Her hand slipped from his grasp, her arm falling to her lap. She slumped forward. He reached out to catch her, but there were scissors in his hand. The blades sliced into her shoulder, cutting her blouse, opening a gash in her flesh.

"Oh, shit, no. Oh, God, I'm sorry." He recoiled, but she tumbled toward him. He twisted away, frantic to keep the scissors away from her body, but fresh cuts opened. Her skin peeled away, showing muscle and bone, but no blood, because she was already dead.

A small hand shook David's shoulder, and the dream lost its vivid colours. Ashley's lacerated body floated before him like a pale ghost. An insistent voice said, "David! David, it's just a dream." But he couldn't quite wake up.

The shaking stopped, and the spectral Ashley closed in again. David moaned.

A hand stroked his head, brushing along his forehead, small fingers smoothing his hair. The cushions shifted and David felt the warmth of another body against his back. Two bare feet nestled against his heels and an arm slid across his chest. Gentle fingers caressed his shoulder, and a familiar voice murmured, "It's okay, David. It's all right. It's just a dream. It's okay, honey. Shh."

Ashley's mutilated form faded into invisibility. David whimpered one last time, then reached up and clung to the arm across his chest. The arm tightened and he sank back into sleep.

Twelve

Hunger woke David. Kim lay cradled against his chest, snoring softly. He kept himself still, breathing in the smell of her hair. Her limbs were entangled with his, one warm bare knee between his legs, a heel hooked around his calf.

The fireplace glowed faintly, a warm counterpoint to the cool wash of a streetlight coming through the picture window. No trace of dawn showed, but David felt wonderfully refreshed. A faint smell of woodsmoke brought back echoes of winter evenings talking and laughing with Aaron and Ashley. The room felt safe. It felt like home.

He worked one arm free. The tension was gone from Kim's features. He brushed the back of one finger delicately across her smooth cheek, and she smiled in her sleep.

This is wrong. With Kim snuggled against him it was impossible to heed the cold voice in his head, but it continued to reproach him. *You're holding onto her because she reminds you of Ashley. She's holding onto you because of a schoolgirl crush.*

Shut up, David told the voice. He tucked the blankets around Kim's shoulder. *Don't wreck this for me.*

It isn't real.

He looked at the sleeping girl. *It feels real.*

The voice didn't respond, except with a palpable skepticism.

I don't care. My life is measured in moments now. This moment feels right. In fact, it feels perfect.

A grumble from his stomach turned his attention to more practical concerns. He took his time easing his right arm from under Kim's head and extricating his legs. He was in no hurry. Sliding a leg from under her smooth, soft calf was not an experience to be rushed.

The room was cold, the floor colder. He put his socks on, grabbed his jacket, and padded into the kitchen. *Aaron won't mind if I raid the fridge.*

A couple of minutes later he was wolfing down a thick sandwich and a glass of water. He was in just as much trouble as the day before, but he couldn't suppress a buoyant good mood. He felt like whistling, but his mouth was full.

When the sandwich was done, he crept back into the living room. He crossed to the picture window and opened a gap in the curtains.

The house stood on a quiet, narrow street lined with shaggy old trees. It all looked comfortable and homely, from Aaron's old Civic in the driveway to the even older Volvo parked in the street.

Nothing that looks like a cop car. He stepped back from the window just in case, sighing as the stress of being hunted came seeping back. *How long until the cops show up here? Aaron used to be a friend, after all. But they think I killed his daughter. They won't expect me to come to him for help.*

Unless Bagwell called them, and they notice that Aaron lives two blocks from the diner.

His stomach gave an unhappy twinge as he thought about Nathan Bagwell. *What's he doing right now? With any luck he's in a hospital with his leg in a cast. Or home, asleep, waiting for the cops to find me.*

David, remembering the passionate fury in Bagwell's face, the mindless, implacable pursuit, knew he would not be so lucky. *He's looking for me right now. He's not going to stop.*

He paced, faint creaks coming from the floorboards. *Bagwell's probably outside the diner right now, freezing his fat ass off, waiting for me to come back. What else can he do?*

Well, he knew about Ashley. Did he know where she lived?

It was possible, David realized. The Bagwells had lived in the neighborhood. It was how Ashley and Cameron had met. *Nathan went past the diner last night. He probably still lives nearby.*

He looked at the window. *Stop it,* he told himself. *It's the middle of the night. Nobody's lurking outside, waiting for you to show up so they can murder you. Go back to bed.*

It was good advice, but he ignored it. He peeked outside, saw nothing, called himself a fool, and pulled the curtain wider so he could peer down the street.

Something moved in the parked Volvo.

"Oh, fuck." He stared, stomach sinking, as a face appeared in the passenger window of the car. The face vanished, the driver's door opened, and a burly figure climbed out. He limped as he came around the front of the car and glared at the house.

Nathan Bagwell.

"Bloody hell. Kim! Wake up!"

Bagwell charged toward the house. David stood frozen, weighing his options, trying to think. The doorknob rattled. The house shook as Bagwell threw his shoulder against the door. Kim gave an alarmed squeak.

"Don't move." David circled the couch, sat down on a coffee table, and put on his shoes. "He's only interested in me."

The door thumped every few seconds. Each impact sent vibrations through the floor and into David's feet. Kim stared at him, a blanket pulled up to her nose, only her wide, frightened eyes showing.

David stood as the front door crashed open. Nathan Bagwell stumbled inside, his puffy jacket flapping. David took a couple of steps toward the kitchen, but Bagwell moved to intercept him. A thick hand plunged into the jacket and pulled out a long shape wrapped in paper towel. With one quick shake the paper towel flew free.

It was a butcher knife, a big one. Bagwell's lips curled back from his teeth and he crouched, wiggling the knife.

"Found you," he said, and took a slow, cautious step toward David.

Kim sat up. Bagwell glanced at her—and froze. The knife drooped in his hand. "Ashley?"

David darted past him and into the kitchen. He reached the back door and paused when he didn't hear pursuit. "Bagwell? Are you coming?"

Footsteps slammed against the floorboards, Bagwell burst into the kitchen, and David tore open the back door. Or tried to. He spent a bad moment fumbling with the bolt and a safety chain that hadn't been there when Ashley was alive.

Bagwell came at him, collided with a chair, and crashed onto the floor. The door opened at last and David fled into the yard.

Where he paused again, despite the panic that tugged him forward. *I can't leave him alone with Kim and Aaron.*

The screen door swung open. Bagwell stood there, knife in hand. A light came on in the house behind him, and a frozen fist closed on David's heart.

Blood gleamed on the tip of the knife in Bagwell's right hand.

More blood covered the back of his left hand, welling from a gash just above his thumb. David whirled and ran, relief making him light-footed as a dancer. *He cut himself with his own knife when he fell.*

David cleared the picket fence in one jump and ran down the alley. He glanced over his shoulder as Bagwell charged the fence like a demented bull. The top rail hit him at waist height and he bent, tumbled over, and landed on his shoulder in the alley. He rose, bleeding from a fresh cut on the temple, and began to run.

David put his head down, tucked in his elbows, and sprinted for all he was worth.

He was pulling ahead when a cramp knifed into his side and made him stagger. He was close to Pat's Place, and he imagined running inside and locking the door. Bagwell, he figured, would come right through the glass.

On his right was a familiar board fence. Mrs. Koslowski's fence, which had done such a poor job of protecting her carrots. David veered over, threw his shoulder against the loose board, and tumbled into her garden.

An instant later Bagwell hit the gap. He was too fat to squeeze through, but he gamely hurled a shoulder into the space. And he stopped, stuck, a foot from David's prone form.

David got to his feet, panting, and thought about trying to subdue or disarm the man. But Bagwell had wisely hit the gap with his right shoulder. His arm stretched into the garden, the blade slicing furiously at the air.

David looked into Bagwell's face, red as borscht and bulging with rage. Strings of spittle flapped outward with every breath. He roared, wordlessly, like a chainsaw beginning to jam.

I guess we won't be talking things out. David looked around the garden, hoping to see a shovel or a rake, something he could use as a weapon. *I could stand here and taunt him. Maybe he'll have a heart attack.*

The next board in the fence creaked. Bagwell came an inch or two closer.

David said, "Well, it's been lovely, but I've got to go."

Two blocks later, David jogged down the middle of the street, watching the sky lighten with approaching dawn. Bagwell lumbered along about forty feet back, not falling behind, not catching up. His face was the brightest red David had ever seen on human skin, and he began to hope the man might suffer some sort of rupture.

Their pace was barely above a brisk walk. David's whole body hurt, and spots danced in front of his eyes while he fought for air. Bagwell was obviously in similar straits, but the man just wouldn't quit.

Pat's Place was behind him now. So was a gas station and one of the city's last pay phones. If he stopped he would be dead before he could finish dialling 911.

The street rose, climbing a small hill, and the pursuit slowed to an absurd pace. The two of them staggered upward until David reached the crest. The rising sun distracted him from burning limbs and lungs. A thin crescent of light gilded rooftops, glinted on the roofs of cars, and lit a few straggly clouds in orange and red. Plumes of vapour rose here and there from chimneys. David let his feet find their own way and drank in the sight.

His last day of freedom. Too much sewage was hitting the air circulation machinery for him to stay at large much longer. Before the sun came up again he would be dead or incarcerated or made catatonic by drugs. This might be his last dawn ever.

Abruptly he was fed up with Bagwell for spoiling a lovely morning. The road descended and David picked up speed. Behind him, Bagwell slowed as he neared the crest.

David shot a glance over his shoulder. He could just see Bagwell's head over the top of the hill. A couple of steps later, the man was out of sight. David glanced around, seeing places on either side where he could dart between houses and reach an alley.

A shiny red pickup truck glittered in a driveway. David ran over, put his hands on the side of the box, jumped, and wriggled into the truck. Then he fought with every ounce of will to control the sound of his breath.

It was hardly necessary. Bagwell sounded like a malfunctioning vacuum cleaner, every agonized gasp so loud he wouldn't have heard gunfire. David lay sprawled on his back, staring up at the brightening sky, hearing Bagwell's wheezing breath coming closer and closer and praying not to see the man's face. Shoes slapped pavement. The feet stopped. Bagwell growled.

The footsteps resumed. David tensed as the sound came closer. He saw a flash of Bagwell's head as the man ran up the driveway.

David kept still. Bagwell would look up and down the alley. When he saw no sign of David he might come back to try the other side of the street.

Best if I wait right here. Besides, I can barely move. He stretched quietly and waited for his breathing to slow down.

Several minutes passed. Birds began to chirp and sing, but there was not yet any traffic noise. The sky was lovely, a soft pink colour slowly deepening into blue. Best of all, David no longer had to run. *Moments. My life is moments now, and this one is pretty good.*

Presently his breathing returned to normal. His lungs ached. His legs ached. He felt frail and shaky. But the burning in his chest was gone. He was over the worst of it.

Slowly, quietly, he bent and straightened his legs, flexing the muscles to keep them from stiffening. *Dear God, I hope I'm done running for my life. But if I'm not, I guess I better be ready.*

A car door clicked shut, and an engine started. Soon commuters would pour out of their homes and into their vehicles. He hadn't heard Nathan for a while. It was time to get moving.

David raised his head, slowly, slowly. With just his nose and forehead above the top of the truck box he scanned the street.

All clear. Cautiously he sat up.

A silhouette rose over the top of the hill. A jogger, in blue track pants and a sweatshirt. A slim figure, running with natural grace, clearly not Nathan Bagwell. David watched warily, ready to duck back down if the jogger came too close.

It was a girl, closing fast, familiar blonde hair waving loose around trim shoulders. David, his exhaustion suddenly forgotten, straightened up and waved.

Thirteen

"Is it bad?" Kim reached the side of the truck and grabbed his jacket in both fists, her eyes wild. "Do you need an ambulance?"

"Running doesn't kill you," he assured her. "It just makes you wish you were dead." She still looked alarmed, so he smiled and said, "I'm fine."

She let go of his jacket and smacked him on the shoulder. "I've been following a trail of blood drops! I thought you were dying."

He laughed, then held up a hand when she got ready to hit him again. "Take it easy. It's Bagwell's blood. The moron cut himself with his own knife." David shook his head. "Twice."

In response she raised one eyebrow, and David had to look away, blindsided by a sudden wave of grief. He looked back when she tugged on his coat.

"Come on. No time to mope."

He clambered out of the truck. As his feet touched pavement he realized why she was in such a hurry.

Beneath the chatter of birds he heard fevered panting, coming closer.

Bagwell's head, shiny with sweat, appeared over the top of the hill. The rest of him rose into view as he climbed. When he saw David he growled, sunlight glinting on the knife as he lumbered forward.

David and Kim backed away, and Bagwell put on speed, moving just faster than a brisk walk. His arms thrashed, the knife brushing his thigh.

"Jesus," David said, "he's going to cut himself again."

"Save your breath for running." Kim turned and jogged away.

Maybe it would hurt less to get stabbed. David shot a resentful glance at Bagwell, then turned and followed Kim.

"You know," she said as he caught up, "you've really let yourself go."

David, without enough breath to reply, settled for giving her a dirty look.

She glanced back. "Well, you're slow, but you're faster than him. Come on." She turned up a side street and gave David an exasperated look when he fell behind.

They were back among condos and blocky apartment buildings. Kim looked over her shoulder, then grabbed a handful of his sleeve. She dragged him across a lawn and between a couple of buildings. In the alley David sagged against a parked van.

"Was that Bagwell's brother? What's his name, Nolan?"

"Nathan." David gave her his best quizzical look, because he didn't have the breath to ask her a question.

"They came to the house once." Her lip curled as she remembered. "It was weird. I guess Cameron wanted his brother along for moral support." She jerked a thumb in Nathan Bagwell's general direction. "That one just stood there on the sidewalk and stared at the house while Cameron came up to the front door. Ashley wouldn't let him in, and she wouldn't go outside. So they talked through the screen door. Or he talked, and then she shut the door and he stood there and yelled for a while." She rubbed her arms as if she were suddenly cold. "I can't believe I thought it was you. That guy was unbalanced."

An engine hummed, and she peeked past the front of the van. "Cop car."

David straightened and leaned over her shoulder. At the mouth of the alley the back fender of a car vanished.

"Let's go." Kim hauled on his jacket, and they hurried across the alley, going in the opposite direction from the cops. They crossed another street, moved between two more buildings, and stopped in another alley.

"They're probably looking for that lunatic, not you." She gave David a sharp look as he lowered himself onto the concrete back step of an apartment building. "Don't sit. You'll stiffen up. Walk around a bit."

He glumly obeyed.

"But keep low. You're still Public Enemy Number One."

"Maybe ...." He coughed, rubbed his aching chest, and started again. "Maybe I should flag down the next cop car. Turn myself in."

She looked at him, her eyes filled with something close to panic. "They'll lock you up again!"

"I'm lucid now. I'll finally get a trial. They can't convict me if I'm innocent, right?"

"What if they drug you? What if they put you back in that awful place?" When he started to speak she said, "No. We can't take that chance. You don't think innocent people get locked up?"

"I—"

"You don't know what it was like." Her face clouded. "After Ashley died. Her face was all over the Internet. In the papers. On TV. She was so pretty. So young. People were furious." Her eyes stared through him, into the past. "They wanted blood. They wanted punishment. They wanted you locked away forever."

"But I'm not—"

"It doesn't matter!" she said fiercely. "They have you. They can't let you be innocent."

He lifted his hands in a helpless shrug. "I can't just keep running."

"I know." She stepped in close, gripping his jacket and pressing her face against his chest. Her voice low and muffled, she said, "I only just found you. I'm not ready to lose you. Not yet."

Moments. Moments like this. How many more will you get? "Me neither."

She stepped back, sniffed, and wiped her eyes. "What happened?"

He gave her a blank look.

"That night," she said. "The night of … the murders."

A forearm under his chin, pushing his head up and back. Trying to backpedal, but there was something behind his heels, probably a cop's foot. Falling. A brutal, jarring impact as he landed, his skull bouncing against pavement. Strong hands on his arms, pinning him, flipping him over. A knee on the side of his head, pressing his face into the asphalt. The cold bite of handcuffs on his wrists ....

He shook his head. "I don't know. I don't remember it at all." He shivered. "I don't want to remember it, either."

Kim gave him a sympathetic look. "I know. But you have to."

His hands shook, and he shoved them in his pockets. "Why, for God's sake?"

"Because what if you have an alibi?"

The question startled him, interrupting his rising distress. "What do you mean?"

"I bet the cops never checked." She sounded fierce, excited. "They were so sure it was you. And there was no trial, so they never had to prove it."

"But—"

"Ashley died on a Wednesday." Some of the animation went out of her voice as she said it. "Cameron died in the hospital. We don't know for sure when he got stabbed. But Ashley's time of death was half past seven, give or take fifteen minutes." Tears glittered on her eyelashes. She ignored them. "You got arrested at a quarter to ten."

"Okay ...."

"So where were you for two hours? Who says you were there when she died? For all we know, you showed up an hour later." Her hands chopped at the air. "What if you were, I don't know, at work until eight? Or hanging out with friends, or on the phone with your mom?"

You were supposed to protect me. He ignored the accusing voice as best he could.

"Then you went over to the apartment, and Cameron was still there. Or Nathan and Cameron." She glanced in the general direction of the street where they'd left Nathan Bagwell.

"You think he's involved?"

She gave him a withering look. "How many homicidal nut jobs do you think this city has? Cameron always brought his brother along when he went to see Ashley. You think he left him behind, that day?"

David considered this scenario. "So ... what? I fought both of them? I stabbed Cameron, and Nathan stabbed me?"

"Maybe." She shrugged. "Maybe Nathan killed his own brother."

"Umm ...."

She arched her eyebrows. "Don't give me that look. He's obviously crackers. They attack Ashley, Nathan gets carried away, he kills her. Then, either Cameron wants to protect her, or Nathan needs to kill Cameron because he's a witness."

"Then why is he mad at me?"

"Same reason Cameron was mad at Ashley because he," she made air quotes, "made him smash her stuff. I'm serious, by the way. He was furious with her. Because he lost his shit and went on a rampage. Ripped her jeans in half. He stomped on her phone until it broke in half. I didn't know you could even do that. And he blamed her. Said she made him do it."

She lifted her hands, fingers curled into indignant claws. "He didn't like what happened. It can't be his fault, so it must be her fault. I bet his brother is the same way. Cameron's dead. It's all your fault because you went out with Ashley and made her happy, so she wouldn't go back to Cameron. You made Nathan kill his brother. QED."

"QED?" he said blankly.

"Exactly."

Maybe I have an alibi. It was a seductive thought. *If there was proof I was innocent. Actual proof. I'd never have to go back.*

Kim grabbed his hand in both of hers and tugged. "Come on."

He followed her down the alley. "Where are we going?"

"We need to jog your memory."

"I don't want to jog."

That earned him a twisted finger. "You need to go home."

"Won't the cops be watching the house?" He tried to resist the pull on his hand, and failed completely. "The last thing I want is to see my parents."

"Not your house. Your apartment. You need to remember that day. We'll start with where you woke up."

He gave in and walked with her. The streets filled with cars as morning rush hour began. David wanted to keep to alleys and quiet side streets, but Kim led him to the busiest street she could find. "We stand out too much in back alleys. We need people to blend in with." She tapped the side of her nose. "It's the first rule of sneaking around. Don't look like you're sneaking around."

He hid his skepticism and went along with it, fighting the urge to flinch each time a car went past. He squared his shoulders and swung his arms a bit, trying to look relaxed.

"That's it," Kim said, and gestured to one side. "This way."

"But that's a quiet street."

She nodded. "But your apartment is this way."

I should know this. I must have gone back and forth between my apartment and Aaron's house. He looked around. They were skirting the south edge of downtown. The street looked familiar, but so did every cross street. Kim, however, seemed to know where she was going.

"Wait a minute." He stopped. Kim kept going, so he trotted after her. "Wait. How do you know where I used to live?"

"Well, I don't know exactly. I can get you within a block. I'm hoping you'll recognize something, once we get close."

He walked along, mulling this over. "How do you know even vaguely where I lived?"

She shrugged. "Ashley said you were the most convenient boyfriend ever. She said you lived a block away from the Plaid Platypus."

David stumbled.

Kim stopped. "What is it? What's wrong?" Her eyebrows rose. "Why are you grinning like an idiot?"

"Moe's Tavern," he said.

By the look on her face she didn't know whether to be amused or concerned. "David, Moe's Tavern isn't real."

"Smartass. Moe's Tavern is what I used to call it. Because Moe worked there. He was a bartender."

She folded her arms. "And Moe is ...?"

"My best friend." His grin faded. "I've been trying to remember where he lives. A phone number. Anything. He worked at the Platypus for years, and I forgot." He pressed a palm against his forehead. "There's so many holes. There's more holes than ... than not-holes."

She caught his wrist and pulled his arm down. "It's okay." She held his hand, her thumbs massaging the base of his thumb. "You'll remember. You'll remember everything."

He shivered.

"Let's keep going." She tugged him into motion. "Walking will warm you up."

Screaming, twisting against the handcuffs, kicking wildly when the cops tried to lift him to his feet. Pain in his wrists, pain radiating from the back of his head, all of it trivial compared to the white-hot agony in his stomach.

More pain than he would have believed the world could hold, and it wasn't enough to blot out the sight of Ashley ....

"David? Are you all right?"

Please, God, don't make me remember.

He squeezed her hand, careful not to hurt her. She matched his grip, her fingers warm and strong. He focussed on the sensation. *Be in this moment.*

"It's okay." Her free hand rubbed his arm. "Everything's okay."

Easy for you to say. You didn't find her body. He smelled dirty socks and curry, saw the walls of her apartment around him, decorated with the covers of classic vinyl albums put up as improvised posters. The corridor was littered with clothing. Ashley, amazing in so many ways, could be a real slob. He called her name, then reached her bedroom door and pushed it open.

"Hey!" Kim yanked hard on his hand. He stopped, and a bus went past in front of him, close enough that the wind ruffled his hair. The stink of exhaust washed over him, banishing the dirty sock smell. The apartment faded.

"Stay with me," said Kim. "It's okay."

He nodded, shaking.

"Tell me about him," she said. "Tell me about this bartender."

"Okay." He took a deep breath and let it out slowly, releasing the last of the horror. "We were friends in high school. I didn't know if it would last after we graduated. But it turned out he wanted to learn how to run."

Fourteen

When the bus reached his stop, David thought about staying in his seat. Standing felt like more effort than he wanted to bother with. Moe was waiting, though, and it was too late to cancel.

So he heaved himself up and left the bus, standing on the sidewalk with drooping shoulders, wishing he'd stayed in bed. *Wimp. Loser. What's wrong with you? Why don't you do Moe a favour and step into traffic? Stop bringing him down.*

Instead, he started to walk. The first few steps were like slogging through mud, but movement and sunshine eroded his lethargy and he picked up his pace. The knowledge that he was late gnawed at him until at last he broke into a run.

Their rendezvous was a dog park with a view of the river valley. A man threw a Frisbee for an excited Golden Retriever. There were no other people in sight, and David slowed, dismay souring his stomach. *You fucked it up. You've only got one friend, and you finally drove him away too.*

"Man, you really need a phone."

David looked around, bewildered, and finally spotted Moe squatting on the far side of a parked car. He had a piece of chalk in his hand, and he was drawing elaborate swirls in the street.

"I have a phone." He circled the car and joined Moe.

"A modern phone. The kind you put in your pocket."

"My phone is always charged," David said. "And I always know where it is. If I lose it, I just go to the wall jack and follow the wire."

Moe looked up long enough to give him a pitying glance.

"Sorry I'm late."

Moe flapped his hand dismissively. "Gave me time to finish the verse." He added a last swipe of chalk and stood. "What do you think?"

David made a show of examining the swirl of Persian calligraphy enclosed in a chalk circle the size of a manhole cover. He pointed to a random spot. "You made a spelling mistake."

Moe snorted and jabbed him with an elbow.

"What does it mean?"

"It's a quote from Rumi. The best translation is," he struck a theatrical pose and deepened his voice, "You are not a drop in the ocean. You are the whole ocean in a drop."

"Wow," said David, deadpan. "That's deep."

"Philistine." Moe grinned. "Actually, just between you and me, I can't decide if Rumi was a genius or a windbag." He pocketed the chalk. "Come on. I want to get a circuit in before it rains."

They jogged across the park, then followed a path along the edge of the valley. Sunlight turned the water below into a blazing stripe of silver, but high banks of cloud blotted out the horizon. "I hope it doesn't rain. It'll wipe out your art."

Moe shrugged. "Rumi would say it's more beautiful because it's fleeting." He laughed. "I'm getting as pretentious as he was."

"How's work?"

"Ugh." Moe made a face. "We had a bachelorette party last night. This chick puked in the umbrella stand. She wasn't even the worst one." He glanced at David. "How's school?"

"It's okay."

Moe gave him a skeptical look.

"Actually, I might take a year off. I'm not sure I really want to be a teacher."

They jogged in silence for a while. The park ended, and they followed a strip of sidewalk with mansions on one side and the yawning gulf of the valley on the other. Moe said, "You're lying. I can always tell."

David flushed, hoping it would look like exertion. His dark mood, interrupted by the distraction of banter and exercise, pressed in, threatening to engulf him. "I don't want to talk about it."

Moe shrugged.

"I'm failing, okay?" He ground his teeth. "I have good days when I get a lot done. Everything's great. I feel like I could conquer the world. Then the bad days come and sometimes I don't even go to class."

Moe didn't speak, didn't even look at him.

"I don't know what's wrong with me. I just ...." *I'm just a fuckup. A useless shitbag who needs to stop taking up valuable classroom space.* "I don't know what to do."

"University's not everything," said Moe. After high school he'd spent a few months doing landscaping, lost his job when winter began, and took a bartending course. It was the only education he planned to get. "You can always take a gap year. Come back when you're feeling better."

There's no point. David didn't bother speaking the words. He poured his attention into running, knowing that if he kept going there was at least a chance he would feel better.

For a while.

Wind buffeted them as the storm drew closer. It would have been chilly if they hadn't been running. The last of the sunlight vanished as they clattered down a long wooden staircase. They ran beside the river, the water dull and grey, the grass colourless. A family darted around a picnic table, packing a cooler, a little girl running after a paper plate that went dancing through the air.

"Here ...." Moe panted, badly winded. "Comes ... the ... wall." He staggered up to the base of another staircase. "You ... ready ... for ... this?"

David didn't answer, just stepped past him and started up the stairs. This was by far the worst part of their weekly run, an endless series of staircases that seemed steeper each time they tackled it. As usual, he cursed himself for dreaming up such a gruelling task. As usual, he kept going.

A glance over his shoulder showed Moe just a few steps behind, face contorted in a determined snarl. Moe could be incredibly driven when he was fixated on a goal. It was almost frightening sometimes. *I wish I had his focus. I might achieve something.*

Litter chased itself in a tight circle on a wooden landing, a plastic bag doing pirouettes at waist height. David swatted it aside and hit the next flight of stairs. Looking ahead would only discourage him. He kept his gaze on the steps just ahead of his feet.

Until lightning flashed, so close that he flinched. The storm was a black wall to his right. Jagged lines of electricity tore through it, thunder crashed like God kicking His celestial garbage cans to the curb, and Moe whooped right behind him.

David whooped along with him. His depression had vanished somewhere during the climb. It was maddening. He couldn't budge his black moods, no matter how desperate he was to escape their grip. With his university education and his dream of a teaching career on the line, he would lie in bed, disgusted with himself, unable to make himself rise. Then something as trivial as a thunderstorm would sweep it all away and he'd be fine.

He reached the top and turned to look at the storm. Moe joined him a moment later, doubling over, hands on his thighs. Tradition demanded they flop down on the grass, vowing never to do this again. The first fat raindrop slapped the railing, though. Moe straightened and started walking, David at his heels.

They trotted across the street and took a walkway between houses, pressing to one side to keep out of the worst of the rain. The next block over, lacking a view of the river valley, held smaller, humbler houses. They followed the walkway to an alley, ran past a couple of yards, and reached Moe's back door. He grabbed a key from under a garden gnome and let them in.

"Mohammed, is that you?" called a voice from the living room.

"Yes, Mom. David is here too."

"Hello, David."

David called, "Hello, Mrs. Pezhman," then followed Moe down the stairs to the basement. He wasn't comfortable upstairs. Everything was too neat. He'd never seen so much as a dirty dish in the kitchen. It made him afraid to touch anything, sure he would break some rule that would seem obvious in hindsight.

Moe's mother was unfailingly pleasant, but she had the most ferocious and forbidding eyebrows he'd ever seen. They were like obsidian knives, one above each eye. Even when she smiled he felt like she was about to announce his execution. He felt guilty at his sense of relief each time he was able to avoid her.

The basement was different. This was Moe's domain, and David loved it. Mrs. Pezhman's influence was obvious—Moe kept the space surprisingly tidy for a man of twenty—but the basement had the air of a boys-only clubhouse.

A heavy bag and a speedbag hung from the ceiling. An air freshener gave off a hint of spice that didn't quite hide a scent of sweat and leather coming from a pair of battered boxing gloves. There was a dartboard on one wall, and posters of young women that stopped just short of being pornographic.

The best part, though, was the cave. Probably designed as a bedroom, the cave was dedicated to movies and games. A vast TV filled one wall. Shelves of DVDs and Xbox games flanked a pair of deep leather armchairs. Squares of paper with delicate swirls of calligraphy decorated the few bits of wall not covered by shelves.

"Coke?" Moe plopped into one chair and opened a bar fridge beside his knees.

"Please." David took the other chair and accepted a can. "What are we watching today?"

"You'll love this." Moe picked up a remote control in each hand. "Kung Fu master versus Muay Thai fighter." He turned on the TV, surfed to YouTube, and did some scrolling. "Here we go."

David settled in to watch, knowing how it would end. Moe loved videos that put traditional martial artists into the ring with professional fighters. To his mind, anyone with a black belt was a self-important buffoon with no idea what real fighting was like.

The video was poor quality, badly lit and shot with a jerky, hand-held camera. David watched politely and grimaced when the Kung Fu master flopped back to land spread-eagled on the canvas.

"Did you see his face?" Moe cackled. "I have to watch that again."

The faces of the fighters were little more than pixelated blurs, but Moe was convinced he saw shock and dismay and terror. He watched the end of the fight in slow motion and laughed in glee.

When it was over he surprised David by turning off the TV. His face went solemn. "I'm worried about you, buddy."

David forced a chuckle. "If I get a black belt, I promise to stay out of the ring."

"Your mood swings are getting worse."

"I ...." David gripped the arms of his chair, feeling his blood pressure climb. "I'm fine."

Moe shook his head. "I think university was good for you. It gave you something to focus on. It kept your mind on the future. I'm worried what'll happen now that you're quitting."

"I don't ...." David's fingers drummed on the arms of the chair. He made himself stop, then watched helplessly as his fingers resumed their dance. "I'm fine. Really."

"Liar." One corner of Moe's mouth twitched up. "I can always tell when you're embarrassed. Don't be." He turned sideways and hooked a knee over one arm of his chair. "You gotta take care of yourself. I need you to keep coming around. You're a good influence."

David gave him a skeptical look.

"Seriously." Moe gestured around the cave. "This is my natural state. Parked on my ass in front of a TV. You think I'd go running if you didn't show up once a week?"

"Whatever," David said. "You're basically a jock."

"And what happens to jocks when they leave high school?" Moe patted the air around his waist, miming an enormous pot belly. "I'm serious. You have this way of ...." His hands moved in incomprehensible swirls as he searched for the right words. "It's like, when I look at the world, it's like this." He held his hands up, palms a foot apart. "You look at the world, and it's like this." His hands flew wide, stretching as far as he could reach.

"You just have short arms, that's all."

Moe laughed. "You're also the funniest person I know. Even when you're depressed, you can still crack me up."

David fidgeted, desperate to change the subject. "Look ...."

"I'm almost done, I promise." Moe looked at David, serious as Death. "You're my friend. You've always been there for me. Now your mood swings are getting pretty bad, and I'm worried about what'll happen if it gets worse and you're alone." He held up a hand as David tried to speak. "So I want you to know you can always come here. You know I can see right through you, right?"

David squirmed.

"So, I'm the one person you can talk to without embarrassment." He smirked. "Because I already know what a dork you are. If things get bad, come see Uncle Moe. Deal?"

He turned away without waiting for a reply, rummaging through the miscellanea on top of his fridge. He produced a couple of game controllers and lobbed one to David. "Now, enough of this chatter. Last week I

149

believe you put a bullet through my kneecap. That was very rude. It's time I got my revenge."

Fifteen

"You can't go in. The cops will be watching."

David leaned past Kim, who stood beside him in the doorway of an office building, and peered down the street. The Plaid Platypus was across the street at the far end of the block. "I think it's closed, anyways. What time is it? What time do bars even open?"

"I don't know. I've never been much of a day drinker." She stepped out of the doorway and turned away from the bar. "Come on. Let's find your apartment."

"What if the cops are watching it, too?"

She shrugged. "You don't live there anymore. It's not like you have a key. Why would you go there?"

Unconvinced, but with no idea what else to do, he followed her. They circled the block, going south.

"I don't see any apartments. Any chance you lived above a convenience store?"

"I don't think so."

"Does anything look familiar?"

"No." He stopped. "There." He pointed across the street. "That print shop used to be a cold beer store."

She gave him a look.

"What?" He spread his hands. "I remember more than bars and liquor stores."

"Like what?"

"Um ...." He looked around. "See that red sign?"

"It's another pub."

He nodded. "And I don't remember it at all."

"Well, that's convincing." She turned around. "Come on. We'll go the long way around."

They retraced their steps, circling wide around the Platypus, going one block north. "Now this," she said, "is more like it."

Pre-war houses alternated with two and three-story apartment buildings on a quiet, shady street. David slowed, gazing around.

"Anything look familiar?"

"No." He stopped. "Wait."

"What is it?"

He pointed at a fire hydrant. "I think I recognize this."

"Are you serious?"

He nodded, a memory of pain echoing in one knee. "I was running. I ran into it."

She snickered. "Let me guess. Does this story involve a pub or a liquor store?"

"No," he said, unsmiling.

After an uncomfortable moment of silence he turned away and moved down the sidewalk. "They used to have parties there." He pointed at a second-story balcony. "Every Friday night. They'd blast music for hours. Shit music, too. Grunge."

He stopped when he reached a pair of side by side apartment buildings, nearly identical. "This is it."

"Which building was yours?"

He shrugged.

Kim took his hand and they stood together, looking at the twin buildings. "One of these apartments was yours?"

"No." He grimaced. "It was twenty bucks more a month for a front view. My place was in the back. I got to look at the parking lot."

They walked between the buildings. There were six second-floor balconies, three on each building. David looked from one to another, couldn't remember which was his, and decided it didn't matter.

"What happened to your stuff? Did you have a storage room? Maybe we could find, I don't know, old letters or something. Did you have a photo album?"

"I'm sure it's all long gone by now." Discouragement washed over him, leaving a bitter, chalky taste on his tongue. "Come on." He trudged down the alley.

"Where are we going?"

It doesn't matter. "We need to go before Mr. Simmons shows up."

"Who?"

"He was the resident manager." David could hear a growing bleakness in his own voice. "He'd remember me. I was always late with my rent."

Kim started to speak, but he ignored her, plodding past garbage bins, smelling piss and rotten food. Every memory that came to him was ugly. Finding roaches in his apartment and knowing he couldn't afford to move.

Cringing at a knock on his door, hanging his head and mumbling excuses to Simmons. Spending five whole dollars on a cherry pie at Safeway, cursing himself for wasting money, then stopping halfway through cutting the first slice, too full of self-loathing to eat.

Kim walked beside him, both of them silent. They came to the end of the alley, where a half-circle of low concrete traffic barriers blocked access to the next street. The concrete made a decent bench, and David plopped himself down. After a moment Kim joined him.

Dark thoughts chased themselves in circles in his mind. His earlier good mood felt as distant as Mars. He wanted to grab Kim's hand, cling to it, beg her to stay with him until the bleak storm inside him finally broke. He wanted to run, to get out of earshot before she could tell him that his gloomy silence was intolerable. Before she could say goodbye.

"Hello!" said Kim, her voice bright and chirpy. "What time do you open?"

He looked at her, startled. She was turned away from him, holding a cell phone. He felt a flash of annoyance that was immediately tempered by Ashley's mocking laughter, echoing in his head. *What's the matter, David? She's not wallowing in your angst with you? She's not patting you on the head while you feel sorry for yourself?*

Ashley always knew how to ruin a perfectly good bad mood.

"Do you know if Moe is working today?" There was a long pause. "Mohammed. Everyone calls him Moe. He used to be a bartender there." Another pause. "I don't know. He was Arabic."

"Persian," David muttered. She ignored him.

"Okay. Thanks." She lowered the phone and looked at him. "No one named Moe works at the Platypus. No Mohammed, either. There's a couple guys from India but no Arabs." When he opened his mouth she said, "No Persians either."

He deflated. The dark swirl of his thoughts, momentarily interrupted, threatened to return. It was an old pattern that had ruined more than a few afternoons with Ashley. *I can't let it spoil my last morning with Kim.*

"You know," she said, "it's the twenty-first century."

He gave her a look. "Yes. I was aware."

She waved her hand at the neighborhood around them. "So why are we doing this the analogue way? What are we, my dad?"

He didn't say, 'This was your idea.'

"We can't get into your old apartment. We can't get your stuff. It's gone. But the real world is online anyway. And digital lasts forever."

He opened his mouth.

"Don't contradict a lady. It's rude."

He closed his mouth.

"I don't remember what I did on a particular day even a month ago. But I can tell you." She held up her phone. "I've got calendar appointments from, like, 2011. I've got emails that go back to when the Simpsons were still funny."

"What are you trying to say?"

She put a hand on his arm and said solemnly, "I'm sorry, David. The Simpsons aren't funny anymore."

"You know, I'm trying to feel grumpy here. You're not helping."

"Sorry," she said, poker-faced. "Would it help if I made fun of your hair? Somebody needs to."

He laughed in spite of himself. "You ...." *You remind me so much of Ashley.* "You are a pest."

"Anyway," she said, suddenly businesslike, "what did you use for a calendar program?"

"I ...." He frowned as he tried to remember.

"Did you have an iPhone?"

"No."

"Android?"

"I ... don't think I had a cell phone. I think I had a land line."

Her eyebrows climbed her forehead. "Even my dad has a cell phone."

"My dad didn't believe in them. My sister only got a cell after she graduated from high school. When I moved out, I didn't have any money. So I got a land line. It was cheaper."

She gave him a look full of baffled pity.

"I had a computer," he said. "I had some kind of calendar program on it."

"Was it online?"

"Why would I need it online?"

"Right," she muttered. "Why put things online when you have to be home to use the Internet?"

He gave her a hurt look.

"Sorry. I shouldn't make fun of your Amish heritage. It was culturally insensitive of me." Before he could find a sufficiently biting reply she said, "You did have email, right? Surely that was online."

He nodded uncertainly. "I, um, don't think I remember my email address."

"No worries." She tapped at her phone. "Ashley used to send me the most God-awful puns. She'd copy everyone. You included." A finger wagged as she scrolled. "Hang on. Okay, here's one." She peered at the phone. "Nope. She didn't copy you on that one. Kind of a girl joke."

There was more scrolling. "Okay. Got one. Wow. I can't believe she sent this to me. I was sixteen." She glanced at David. "My sister totally corrupted me."

He made an impatient gesture.

"David four three two at cyberianorth dot com."

"That's it," he said. "I remember!"

"Don't get too happy. You still have to remember your password."

He squeezed his eyes shut, lifted his hands, and imagined a keyboard. *Come on, David, you must have typed your password a thousand times.*

"Cyberia North," she said. "This might be the dorkiest site on the Internet. When was the last update, 1985?" Then, after a moment, "Okay, I found a login page." She murmured each letter in his username as she typed it in.

"So. Any chance you remember your password? I bet it was something lame. I'm gonna try *DavidLovesAshley4Ever.*"

He made his voice deep and ominous. "Klaatu barada nikto!" In a more normal tone he added, "The 'tu' is a digit."

She gave him a blank look.

"Oh, for heaven's sake. Does nobody watch the classics anymore?" He took the phone from her and entered his password. Email subject lines filled the screen. "Wow."

Kim tried to grab the phone. "What is it?"

"Asian women want to meet me for romance and marriage." He snickered. "Oh, and I may already qualify for a loan."

She made another grab for the phone, and he evaded. "All right, all right." He scrolled through five long years of junk mail. "What was the date of ...." He hesitated, not wanting to say the words. "What date am I looking for?" As she started to answer, he held up a hand. "Wait. I think I found it."

He scanned the last handful of messages before his inbox turned to spam. There was an email from Moe, the subject line 'Movie Night'. Two from Ashley that looked like forwarded jokes. A reminder about a dental appointment, a credit card statement, and something from admin@NewDawn with 'Policy Update' for a subject.

Kim crowded against him, not an unpleasant sensation, and peered at the screen. He said, "I really don't want to know what the balance is on that credit card."

"Look." She pointed, the tip of her finger obscuring whatever she was pointing at. "You have a 'Saved Mail' folder." When he didn't respond she poked the screen.

A new list of messages appeared. Four of them were from Ashley, with subjects like 'Love U' and 'Happy Birthday Hunk'. The fifth message was from Susan2005 with a subject of 'Finally scanned this'.

He ran a finger along the edge of the phone, found a button, and pressed it. The screen went dark. His hand shook as he gave the phone back to Kim.

"It's all right," she said in a small voice. "I still get ambushed by it. I'll be fine for weeks. Months, sometimes. Then something stupid just brings it all back, and I start crying. Something trivial. A song she liked. A song she hated. Some kid wearing a dress like she used to wear when I was six." She linked her arm through his and rubbed his shoulder. "Sometimes I can shake it off in a minute or two. Sometimes I bawl my eyes out."

It wasn't the emails from Ashley that had triggered him. He figured if he ever re-read them he would, as Kim said, bawl his eyes out. But something else had pushed his buttons. He wasn't sure what. All he knew was that his heart was racing, the blood roaring in his ears. He focussed on the warm pressure of her hand on his shoulder until the roar faded.

When he was calm she said, "What was your job, before ...?"

The room was small, the desks too big for the children. He stood frozen in the doorway, knowing he had to flee before they realized he had no idea what he was doing. But a woman was speaking, pointing at him. "Children, this is David. He'll be helping you. David, come in and meet the class."

"I think I was a teacher." He rubbed his forehead. "No, that can't be right. I was a tutor. I didn't have my degree yet." *You weren't ever going to get your degree.* "But I had some education courses. I got a job with a tutoring company."

"How late did you work?"

He drummed his fingers on the concrete barrier, trying to pull an answer from the tangle of memories. "I don't know." He shifted, and discovered that one leg had gone to sleep. He stood, hobbled in a circle, and hissed as pins and needles danced up the back of his leg.

Kim stood and brushed off her rear end. "What do you think? How can we find your old work schedule? I'll do a search for tutoring companies in Calgary."

"Ice cream."

Kim gave him an odd look. "Come again?"

"We went for ice cream this one time." He spoke slowly, piecing the memory together. "It was cold. I didn't really want ice cream. I couldn't afford it. But Ashley really wanted to go."

Kim watched him silently.

"They had this bulletin board." He could see every detail, the empty shop, the snow on the ground outside. "I was looking for job ads. Something I could do in the evenings. But Ashley didn't want me to get another job. She said I was already stressed enough. She worked weekends. She said evenings were the only time she got to see me. She said, it's only money. It's not important."

She was being kind. What she really meant was, you can't handle another part-time job. You can barely handle the job you've got. You flunked out of university, you're late for work more often than you're on time, and your depression is getting worse. And she was right.

"So ... you didn't work late, then?"

"It was an after school thing. Sometimes we'd run sessions during the day, like on PD days. But they always closed by six."

He watched her absorb this information. He watched her droop. Then her shoulders rose. "I'm not giving up." She glared at him, as if daring him to argue. "I'm not done with you yet. Understand?"

He said meekly, "Yes, ma'am."

Her eyes narrowed. "That's the spirit," she said at last. "Okay. If you weren't at work, maybe you were with your friend. Moe."

"But he's not there!" David gestured in the direction of the Platypus. "I don't know how to find him."

"We'll go to his house."

"I don't remember his address!"

"Such a defeatist attitude." She took out her phone. "How many off-leash parks do you think there are, right along the edge of the river valley?" She pecked at the screen, not waiting for an answer. "Think you could find your way from the park?"

"Maybe?" When she shot him a hard look he said, "Yes. Absolutely. No problem."

"Good." She put her phone away. "Let's go."

Sixteen

"Jesus. What happened?"

Kim, standing with David where the foot path from the park met the alley, gave him a quizzical look.

"That's his house." He nodded at a crumbling board fence, the middle sagging to almost 45 degrees. "It's really gone to shit."

"I don't see any cops." Kim peered up and down the alley. "There's a van back there." She looked at David, then at the sagging fence. "I could go knock on the door."

"Hell with it," he said, and stepped into the alley. "If there's cops in the van, they've already seen me."

Moe's back gate was missing. The yard was a mess, a rusty rake lying on the ground, empty flower pots and bits of garbage scattered around. The lawn was a lumpy brown mat underfoot, the withered strands of grass at least a foot long.

They must have moved. How will I find him now? He looked at the house, wincing. The windows were filthy. The flowerbeds by the back door, once so meticulously maintained, were choked with last year's dead weeds.

And a familiar garden gnome, lying on its side.

"Oh, hell." He looked around the yard, recognizing a grimy patio table surrounded by toppled chairs. "They're still here."

"That's good, right?"

He ignored her, walking to the back door and nudging the gnome with his foot. There was no sign of the spare key. He used his toe to stir the weeds, then gave up and opened the screen door. He knocked.

The inner door creaked and swung inward.

"Hello?" David nudged the door farther open and leaned in, wrinkling his nose at the smell of spoiled food. "Moe? Mrs. Pezhman?" He knocked again, then stepped inside.

A sweatshirt lay on the stairs leading up to the kitchen. The basement stairs were dark, and no light came on when David flicked the switch. He shrugged and walked upstairs, stepping over the shirt.

The kitchen was a horror show, dirty dishes filling the sink and spreading across the counter. The table was invisible under a layer of takeout containers and plates furry with mold. Kim pushed past him, hurried to the window, and opened it. She leaned close to the screen, breathing in fresh air.

The living room was gloomy, curtains drawn, every window closed, the air heavy with dust. A pizza carton lay in the middle of the floor. A pair of boxer shorts were draped over the back of the sofa. Moe, apparently, was living alone.

"Stay away from the front windows," he said to Kim, and headed down a hallway. There was a doorway on either side, rooms he had never seen. Now, for the first time, the doors were open. He peeked into the first room, then grunted, surprised.

The converted bedroom was now a sewing room, and it was immaculate. A table held a pair of sewing machines. Fabric in rolls and bundles filled a set of shelves. There were cabinets with countless little plastic drawers. Everything was perfectly tidy.

When he pushed the door farther open, dust swirled on the floor. A closer look at the table showed a thick film of dust on the tabletop and both sewing machines. It was profoundly depressing, and he closed the door behind him as he left.

The room across the hall was a bedroom, just as tidy as the sewing room and just as unused. A rack in the corner held dresses on hangers. Several pairs of women's shoes made a tidy row underneath. Everything was covered in dust.

I never really knew you, Mrs. Pezhman, but you always smiled when I came over. Rest in peace.

He found Kim at the back door, lips twisted in a grimace. She looked like she wanted to bolt outside, but when he started down the basement stairs, she followed.

The downstairs lights worked, but he almost wished they didn't. The basement was a mess. At least there was no food, but laundry and random bits of garbage littered the floor. The dartboard and punching bags were gone.

"Ashley would have loved this guy," Kim said. "He's a bigger slob than she was."

"They didn't get along," David said absently. Moe had been almost as dazzled by Ashley as David was, but she had never liked him.

He peeked into the cave. The TV was gone, along with half the DVDs. *Everything that's easy to sell.*

"David." Kim's voice was low and strained. "I found your friend."

Moe's bedroom was next to the cave. A man lay sprawled across the bed, fully clothed, breath whistling through his nose. David and Kim stood in the doorway, held back by the dirty clothes piled on the threshold and by a miasma of body odour so thick it ought to have been visible.

"I thought you said he was a jock."

David looked at the figure on the bed. A stained t-shirt didn't quite cover a broad, flabby stomach. The man's dark hair looked familiar, but not his slack, puffy face.

"He was." David took a breath, stepped over the mound of clothes, and circled the bed. He opened a set of curtains. Sunshine flooded in, lighting the man's face.

It's not him. Relief washed over David, vanishing a moment later when he saw that the dissipated, old-looking man on the bed had a crooked nose. "Jesus fucking wept. Oh, Moe. What happened to you?"

"David."

Something in Kim's voice chilled him. She was staring at his feet. "Don't move."

A syringe lay among a tangle of dirty socks, the tip of the needle pointing up at an angle of thirty degrees or so.

David scanned the detritus around him, saw nothing else that looked dangerous, and squatted.

"Don't touch it. There's opioid shit that can give you an overdose just from touching it. It happens to cops and paramedics sometimes."

He gave her a skeptical look.

"Things changed while you were away."

David glanced at Moe. *Isn't that the truth.* He used a dirty sock to pick up the syringe, then picked his way carefully to the door. He looked around the basement helplessly, finally going to a bookcase and dropping the syringe point-down in a jar Moe had once used for paintbrushes.

Kim put a hand on his shoulder. "I'm sorry."

"I can't believe it. He was ...." David looked around at the ruin of the basement. "Whatever this is, he was the opposite." He gave her a wry look. "I'll tell you one thing. If he's my alibi, he's lost all credibility as a witness."

"I hate to go back in there." Her mouth made a grim line. "But we better go see if he knows anything."

Moe, however, refused to wake up. David shook him until Moe's head flopped from side to side before giving up. "Do you think he needs an ambulance?"

"He's breathing okay." Kim shrugged. "I think he just needs time."

They went upstairs. David flicked the boxer shorts onto the floor and sat on the sofa. Kim joined him.

"Moe was cool."

Kim didn't speak, but he could see her disbelief.

"I'm serious. He was built like a bodybuilder, he was smart, and he had this, I don't know, this intensity. Like nothing was going to stand in his way. I was worried he'd take Ashley away from me."

Kim laughed, a spontaneous, derisive sound that said she found the idea ridiculous. He grinned, pleased.

"You should have seen his face when he met her. He was lovestruck. He screwed it up, though." David thought back, remembering the three of them walking along the edge of the dog park. "He made some crack about how she was wasted on such a skinny guy. How she needed to raise her standards. It was supposed to be a joke. Teasing me, flattering her, pretending to flirt. But she took it the wrong way." He kept his voice light, although the memory was far from pleasant. "Crisis averted. She stayed with me."

He didn't tell her the rest of it. He and Ashley swapping puns, Moe feeling increasingly left out. They were using the river as inspiration, talking about cash flow issues when you put money in the wrong kind of bank, when Moe blurted, "Why don't hipsters wade in rivers? It's too mainstream!"

Ashley gave him one of the cool, mocking looks she was so good at. "Thanks for contributing." Her voice dripped condescension. "Maybe you should stick to lifting weights." To David she said, "The key to a good river pun is going with the flow. You have to stick with the current topic, right?"

Moe stared at her, stung, as she serenely ignored him. He turned and stalked away, David staring after him until

Ashley nudged him with her elbow and they resumed their walk.

He never brought the two of them together after that.

The dusty living room began to feel intolerable. David stood up and paced, Kim watching silently from the sofa. He sniffed, decided he couldn't stomach the smell of rotting food for another minute, and went into the kitchen. He found garbage bags, filled two of them with leftover food and takeout containers, and set them outside the back door. Then he washed dishes until the drying rack was full. He cleaned the counter, then covered it in dirty dishes so he could wash the table. By this time the room was quite cold. He closed the window, then wiped down a chair before sitting.

Kim appeared on the stairs. "Sleeping Beauty is still sleeping."

"Some alibi," he said wearily.

She sat across from him. "I wonder if Nathan Bagwell has one."

"One what?"

"Alibi," she said patiently. "I wonder if someone saw him leaving work with his dirtbag brother right before Ashley died."

He shrugged. "Let's hope the cops take an active interest this time around. They're the only ones who can find out."

"Maybe." She gave him a speculative look.

"It was five years ago!"

"I know. But I can tell you everything I did that day." Her eyes stared past him, haunted. "It's burned into my brain."

"Still ...."

"People remember murders," she said. "If you know the victim. Even if you just know a sibling of the victim." She gave him a pointed look. "I had friends back then who still have nightmares today. They never even met Ashley. But they saw what I went through. They remember that day almost as clearly as I do."

A wave of irrational guilt washed over him. *I was her boyfriend. I was supposed to protect her. I could have prevented so much damage to so many people if I'd only been there in time.*

Where was I?

"Anyway," said Kim, shaking off her dark mood. "Let's start with where he worked." She took out her phone.

"It's hopeless." He regretted the words as soon as they were out, but they were true.

Kim gave him a cold look. "When a close family member gets murdered, your privacy goes to shit." Her lips twisted. "Grief is interesting, don't you know. Pair it with violent death and the vultures come swooping in. Everyone wants to feed on you."

Her thumbs jabbed at the screen of her phone. "There's nothing about Nathan Bagwell." She swiped, jabbed, and swiped some more. "Here we go. Looks like Bagwell's parents got interviewed almost as much as I did."

Long minutes passed while she read. "They don't talk about Nathan. Maybe we can ask them directly." She scrolled. "His father was a mechanic and his mother was a phone psychic." She swiped with her thumb and frowned. "I've got his father's name, but it's John. There's probably a lot of John Bagwells."

"We could start calling garages and repair shops," David said. "It'll take a while, but ...."

"His mother's name is Sunrise Macallister," Kim said. "That one'll be a little easier to find."

"And we can interrogate her for only three ninety-five a minute?"

Kim looked at him, her expression arch. "She worked for AAA Reliable Psychic Hotline. The fine print on their website says they're owned by Nelson Communication Corporation." She pecked at the phone, then turned it, showing him a screen full of tiny text. "The office number is here on the Nelson website."

David shook his head. "Moe was right."

She raised her eyebrows.

"I should have gotten a cell phone." He thought a moment. "I guess you might as well call them."

Kim looked at the phone, then hesitated. "Why would they answer my questions?"

"Because you're Inspector Smith with the Calgary Police, doing a background investigation into everyone associated with the notorious escaped criminal, David Parkinson."

She blinked. "Do the Calgary Police have inspectors?"

"I don't know, and neither will the office drones at Nelson Communications. Don't overthink it. Call already."

"If I get through to his mother, what do I ask her?"

"Start with whether she knows where he was that night. It's a long shot, but you never know. Then ask about how to get in touch with his father, any friends, where he was working, that sort of thing."

Kim nodded, hesitated, then dialed. She quickly found herself on hold. David listened to tinny instrumental music for a minute or so, then stood, restless. He went to the living room, where he paced back and forth until he got tired of watching his step. He gathered up dirty clothes and looked around, wondering where to put them. Finally he carried the whole lot downstairs and dumped it into Moe's washing machine. He picked up enough laundry to fill the machine, added soap, and got the machine started.

When he returned to the kitchen Kim had the phone in her lap, her face inscrutable.

"Well?"

"Nathan was with her that night." She gave him a mournful look. "All afternoon. He got off work at six, and they were watching a movie together and eating popcorn by seven."

He walked over and sat across the table from her. "So where does that leave us?"

"With only one avenue to pursue," she said. She reached across the table and tapped his forehead. "You need to remember what happened."

"I can't just make myself remember things. I've tried."

Her eyebrows descended. She opened her mouth to speak, then froze.

"What?"

She touched a finger to her lips.

Shoes scuffed against concrete outside. Knuckles rapped on the front door.

I don't think we locked the door. David stared at Kim, barely breathing. *Relax. It's probably Mormons or something. Or a salesman.*

"Mr. Pezhman?" It was a man's voice, deep and self-assured. "Open up, please. It's the police."

Kim grabbed David's hand in both of hers. She squeezed hard enough that he opened his mouth in silent protest.

The man outside knocked one more time. David shifted on his chair, ready to spring up.

When the rustle of footsteps came again he didn't move, sure it was his overstressed imagination. Kim rose, though. She moved to the living room and peeked through a gap between the curtain and the window frame. "They're leaving."

David followed her to the living room. He watched a couple of men in suits open the doors of a blue sedan. He held his breath until the car drove away.

The little house felt claustrophobic now, like a cell with the walls pressing too close. He rummaged through drawers looking for a pen, finally going downstairs to the shelf where Moe used to keep art supplies. He found a Sharpie, but no paper. He considered grabbing one of the calligraphy pieces on the wall of the cave but couldn't bring himself to mess with one of the last traces of the old Moe.

In the kitchen he found a receipt for Chinese food, overlooked during his cleaning binge. He flipped it over and scrawled a brief note:

Moe,

FFS pull yourself together. I need your help.

David

He added Kim's phone number and laid the note in the middle of the pristine kitchen table where it would be difficult to miss. He led Kim out the back door, scanning the yard and the bit of alley visible over the sagging fence.

Nothing had changed.

He stepped back into the house and added a line to the bottom of Moe's note.

PS. There's wet laundry in your washing machine.

By the look of the house it would be months before the man noticed on his own.

David returned to the yard, where Kim took his hand and squeezed it. He met her gaze, read the anxiety there, and responded with a grin and a shrug. *Either we're about to be arrested, or we aren't. Only one way to find out.*

They crossed the yard, peeked up and down the alley, then hurried to the pathway between buildings. No sirens blared. No cops sprang out to tackle him. His tension eased with every step. By the time they reached the dog park he was almost relaxed.

They walked along the edge of the river valley, as far as they could get from the street without looking like they were hiding. He gazed at the stripe of water, like a spray of diamonds glittering through the trees, wondering if he was seeing it for the last time.

A car slid to a stop across from the park. The driver opened his door, shading his eyes as he looked toward David. He climbed out of the car, a heavyset figure in a cowboy shirt.

"Oh, shit."

A couple of terriers erupted from the car, running in tight circles around the man's feet. He drew an arm back as if to throw a ball. The dogs dashed pell-mell into the park, the man laughing and lowering his arm as he followed.

David gave Kim a sheepish look. "I thought I saw Nathan Bagwell."

"I still think he did it." There was an edge of desperation in Kim's voice. "His mother's just covering for him."

David shrugged. "Well, it sounds good, but it's not like we can prove it."

She took out her phone, glanced at it, and put it back in her pocket. "Will your friend call? Or will he be mad because we were in his house?"

"Moe has a soft spot for me," he assured her.

Moe's scowling face inches from his own, one strong hand on David's wrist, twisting and shoving him forward. His cheek flattening against plate glass, the door finally swinging open. David, arms churning the air for balance, staggering into the street.

"David? Did you hurt your leg?"

"Huh?" He looked down. He was rubbing one knee, trying to massage away remembered pain. He straightened up. "No. I'm fine."

"What's the plan, then? We try to stay at large until Moe wakes up, and hope he was with you that afternoon?"

David rubbed his forehead. "I think I saw him that day."

She nodded, excited.

"But I didn't stick around." He faced her. "Give me your phone."

"Why?" She took out the phone and handed it to him. "What are you going to do?"

"I'm going to pick off a scab." He stared at the little screen, found he had no idea how to do anything, and gave the phone back to Kim. "Will you bring up my email again?"

She tapped a few times and handed it back. "Pick off a scab?"

"My memory is coming back in bits and pieces. It's still full of holes. But it all stops, I don't know, a few days before the murder." He scrolled through the list of email messages, feeling his blood pressure climb. "Something happened to me. It must have been bad." His mind ran through the ugly things he'd recalled of his life. He sensed this would be worse.

There it is. He stared at the subject line, so innocuous and bland. 'Finally scanned this', from Susan2005. A voice inside his head screamed at him to give the phone back, to fling it away, to smash it.

Instead, he tapped the word *Finally*. The message appeared, and he read the first line.

Dear David,

And it all came back to him.

Seventeen

Freedom, it turned out, wasn't all it was cracked up to be. Moving into his own apartment brought David a couple weeks of giddy euphoria, followed by his first bout of depression. He told himself he was just tired, worn down by a job in a convenience store and the prospect of starting university.

He eked out a living with student loans and dead-end jobs, alternating between delight at the novelty of it all and dismay at the relentless grind of work, study, and poverty.

It became a cycle of euphoria and depression. He learned to study and do as much homework as possible during the upswings, knowing he would barely rise from his couch on the bad days. He wondered if he needed therapy, but in the euphoric phase he couldn't believe he had a problem. Then the weight of an elephant would settle on him, and seeking help became too much bloody work.

The roller coaster was getting worse, the peaks higher and the troughs lower and the cycles coming faster, when Ashley crashed into his life like a meteor and changed everything. A nervous voice deep inside whispered warnings. The pendulum was suspended on the upswing. It had to come down eventually.

He ignored that voice. Life was finally good. He meant to enjoy it.

Every week he thought about getting back in touch with Grandpa. Something inside him shied away, though. Thoughts of his grandfather were charged with too much emotion, with an irrational fear of what Grandpa would think of him. So he put it off.

Every week he swore he would call soon, until an early-morning phone call terminated his period of denial. It was Mom, sounding tearful and afraid. Grandma was in a coma. The family was gathering at the hospital.

Mom facing a crisis was enough to make anyone climb the walls; he could hear her wailing as he stepped off the elevator. David slid silently into Grandma's room and hovered behind Matthew and Emily. He couldn't see the faces of his father, off to the left, or his grandfather, to the right. But he could feel the tension that simmered between the two men.

In the centre of the room lay Grandma, frail and angular under a sheet, bones and veins showing through the loose folds of her skin.

David stared at the floor in quiet misery.

After a while a nurse wheeled in a silver cart and announced in a no-nonsense voice that everyone had to leave for a while. Grandpa turned, his eyes flicking once across David's face. His expression was flat and lifeless. There was no sign of recognition.

The family trickled into the corridor. Mom grabbed David and hugged him. Matt punched him on the arm. Emily smiled and said, "Hi."

David glanced at his father, then did a double-take. Dad was haggard. He looked twenty years older, with deep lines around his mouth and eyes. Every scrap of his blustery confidence was gone.

The morning passed in a dragging agony of waiting. Mom pulled herself together enough to make small talk with David and his siblings. Dad and Grandpa, however, remained tight-lipped and withdrawn.

They stood around in the hallway. They stood around in Grandma's room. They stood around in the lounge area. When Emily finally said she was hungry, David looked in surprise at his watch. And realized that he was very, very late for work.

New Dawn Tutoring was the greatest job he'd ever had. That wasn't saying much; he'd worked some truly shit jobs since moving out on his own. New Dawn paid well, by David's standards anyway. They didn't make him wear a tacky uniform. If his boss held the tutors in contempt, treating them like a necessary evil rather than a skilled resource, at least the work itself felt meaningful.

He worked for several hours each weekday afternoon, starting right after school. He sat with a handful of eight- and nine-year-olds, helping them with whatever subjects they found challenging. It was by turns fun, frustrating, and deeply satisfying.

He was supposed to arrive by three. Students began trickling in at half past three. David reached New Dawn at half past four, breathless and sweating.

Ms. Cleary, owner, president, and tyrant-in-chief, was with David's students. She gave him a single cold glare as she walked out.

David was distracted and unsettled, and the kids sensed it, acting up more than usual. He didn't have his normal reserves of patience. His thoughts kept wandering to his family. He was taking a girl through a math problem for the third time when he realized to his shock that he was yelling. He stopped in mid-sentence as a tight silence filled the room.

Ms. Cleary stood in the doorway. She gave him a frosty glance and moved away. He looked at the girl he'd been yelling at. She was wide-eyed and still. "Sorry," he muttered. "Let's start over."

When the session ended at five, David felt like bolting for the door. Instead he watched the children mill out, then spent a few minutes tidying up. At last he headed for the exit.

"David." Ms. Cleary stood in the doorway to her office. "Don't come into the classroom if you're not prepared to do your job."

She stepped back and closed her office door. David slunk out.

At home he changed into sweats and went outside to run. It usually took five or ten minutes of pounding the pavement for the day's stress to fall away. Today it was tougher. He pushed himself, running harder, craving the sense of exhausted well-being he knew would eventually steal over him.

Faces kept hovering in front of him. Grandma, drawn and ghastly, eyes closed. Grandpa, blank-faced. His father, looking dead inside but somehow still suffering. Ms. Cleary, disapproving. The little girl, startled and hurt when he yelled.

He ran harder. It was getting dark, and tears blurred his vision. He tucked his chin in and pushed himself. He was running out of time to find that zone of peace.

He felt a scream building up inside, and he screwed his eyes shut, legs pumping frantically, teeth gritted in frustration.

He ran into a fire hydrant.

The pain was incredible. His kneecap slammed into a bolt. Momentum sent him catapulting over the hydrant, dragging his shin over the metal, his hands slapping into the asphalt.

The top of his head hit next, mercifully meeting grass. His hips slammed down on concrete. He lay there, paralyzed with pain, unable to draw a breath to scream.

When he finally began to collect himself, he shuddered at what he saw. Flaps of skin hung from the heels of his hands. His right knee was visibly swollen through his sweat pants. Blood from a scraped shin stained the fabric.

He took his time getting up, using the hydrant for support. By the time he was standing it was slick with blood from his torn hands.

After a couple of minutes he found he could take little, hobbling steps. He limped home, leaning where he could on walls or fences. He left a trail of red handprints the entire way.

Once in his apartment he sank onto the couch and just lay there, breathing through clenched teeth, hands cupped against his chest. He wanted to call Ashley and ask her to come over. She would be solicitous, loving, sympathetic. The problem was, he would fall apart. *I can't let her see me blubbering.*

This was Tuesday. They invariably spent Friday nights together. He would suggest they pick a movie and cuddle on the couch. Just the thought of it comforted him immensely. One way or another, things would be all right.

That gave him the strength to rise. He washed and bandaged his hands, then stripped off his sweat pants. His leg was a mess. With the blood washed off it looked a little better, but not much. The scrapes on his shin were minor. His knee, however, was ugly.

The joint still worked, if painfully. He grabbed a bag of frozen corn and flopped onto the couch.

It was a long night, punctuated by only snatches of sleep. Between the noxious swirl of his thoughts and stabs of pain each time he shifted his leg, he spent more time staring at his ceiling than anything else.

Showering and eating breakfast exhausted him. He thought about leaving early for work, maybe treating himself to lunch at a café. *And coffee. Lots of coffee.*

Instead he eased himself onto the couch. *I'll just rest for a minute.*

He woke up with a stiff neck and a sense of rising panic. It was late, past two o'clock. He shaved with reckless haste, changed his shirt, and set off at a fast hobble for the bus.

He was late for work, earning him another chilly glare from Ms. Cleary. He sat down, grimacing and trying to find a comfortable position for his leg.

The children were curious about his bandaged hands and his limp. When he tried to be vague they pounced on it and grilled him. So he had to explain that he had run into a fire hydrant. This sent them into peals of laughter, and they talked about it loudly for a long time.

David was in too much pain to laugh with them. "All right, let's get to work." He stood, hissing with pain as his leg straightened, and took a step.

A girl said, "Watch out for fire hydrants!" and the room erupted in laughter.

"That's enough!" David snapped, and the room went quiet. He limped over to Josh Chan's desk. "What are you working on today, Josh?"

Josh didn't answer. His gaze was fixed on the doorway. David turned his head and saw Ms. Cleary watching him, mouth tight with disapproval. She shook her head and walked away.

It was the beginning of a long, tense afternoon.

Eighteen

When David stopped by the hospital that evening, he was corralled by a young intern determined to examine his leg. By the time he was done David knew for sure that his bones were intact. He also had a bottle of anti-inflammatories in his pocket, two pills dissolving in his stomach, and an elastic bandage around the injured joint. He felt noticeably better as he limped off to Grandma's room.

When he reached her wing the nurse at the station looked up with a frown. "Visiting hours are over, sir."

David's face fell. He had endured a lot of pain and bother to get here, and it was all for nothing.

The nurse's face softened. She said, "Well, I guess you could look in on her. It's your grandmother?"

David nodded, surprised. She smiled and waved him forward.

He entered Grandma's darkened room and sank down on a chair. It was quiet and peaceful in here, and he sighed, stretched his leg out, and let himself relax a bit.

The thousand tiny sounds of a busy hospital faded into white noise. All he heard was the slow, even rasp of

Grandma's breathing. David gazed past her at the far wall and tried to let his mind go blank.

Her breathing stopped.

It took a moment for David to realize. He sat up straight, startled. A buzzer rang somewhere, but the sound somehow wasn't intrusive. David looked at her face, unchanged from a moment ago when she had lived. He remembered his birthday, when she baked and fussed over him. He supposed she had loved him. He was embarrassed that he didn't feel very much at all.

"Good bye, Grandma." He expected drama, doctors rushing in and shouting orders, but only a single nurse appeared, walking to Grandma's bedside as David slipped out.

At the nurses' station he asked to use the phone and dialled a familiar number. A gruff voice said, "Yeah?"

"Dad, it's David."

There was silence on the other end.

"Um, she—Grandma just died."

More silence.

David said, "Bye, Dad," and hung up.

"Is this a millennial thing? You expect your mommy and daddy to hold your hand? Mommy and Daddy aren't here, David. You need to pull up your socks."

David sat in Ms. Cleary's office, seething, fighting to keep his face expressionless. Most of the time Cleary made at least a token attempt to hide her disdain, but today she'd decided to indulge herself.

She droned on, haughty and contemptuous, explaining that, contrary to what he might have imagined, employees have responsibilities, and aren't entitled to a paycheque just because they want one.

He thought back to when he'd found the job posting from New Dawn Tutoring, how excited he'd been, revising his résumé with feverish haste, terrified they'd hire someone else and he'd miss his chance.

Now he knew the company was always hiring, because staff turnover was brutal. Cleary took each resignation as proof she was right. Young people were irresponsible and childish. Every time someone quit, her attitude toward the remaining tutors became even worse.

"Are you listening to me? I said you're a grownup now. It's time you started acting like one. Do you even know what that means?"

It's not my skills that make me a valued employee. It's my high tolerance for humiliation. He ground his teeth and waited for her to wind down.

"You can be replaced, you know. I've had three applications so far this week."

Yeah, right. Three people who would quit inside a week, and you know it.

"Did you just roll your eyes at me?" Her voice rose, becoming shrill. "I won't put up with that kind of attitude!"

Whoops. He thought about apologizing but knew he'd never be able to choke the words out. Not that it mattered. She didn't give him a chance to respond.

"There's a lot of negative entries in your file, you know. Mostly tardiness, but in the last few days your attitude has really become quite intolerable. You've been warned repeatedly." She leaned across her desk, jabbing a finger at him. "You could be fired, young man! What would you think about that?"

He was trying to formulate an answer when she said, "Go! The students are waiting. You'll be late."

As he hobbled out she added, "Again."

He stopped outside the classroom door, closed his eyes a moment, and breathed deeply. *It's going to be okay.* He stepped into the room.

Jacob Tanner, eight years old, was running full-tilt toward the door. He was laughing and looking back over one shoulder. Emma Hughes, the same age, was a step behind him, her face thunderous with indignation. A large spitball fell from her forehead as she ran.

Jacob crashed solidly into David's bad leg. The world went red with pain, and when the haze cleared Jacob was backing away, eyes wide. "Sorry." He backed into Emma, but his eyes never left David's face. "Sorry."

The whole class, David realized, was staring at him. *Jesus, what do I look like?* He hastily smoothed his features. "Sit down, please, Emma."

Jacob was already in his seat. Emma hurried to her own chair, and David looked around the room. "What are we working on today?"

He did his best to maintain at least a façade of serenity, but the visible discomfort of the children told him he was failing. His knee throbbed with every beat of his heart.

This will pass, he told himself. *You just need to get through a few more hours.*

When a boy named Noah brought out a sketchpad and a couple of pencils, David saw his chance to focus on something calming and low-stress. He took a seat beside the boy. "Wow. I can't believe an art teacher gave you homework."

Noah scowled, and otherwise ignored him.

David watched him work for a couple of minutes. The boy drew a rectangle with several more rectangles inside it. Only when he added legs to the bottom of one shape did David recognize it. "Is that the front of the classroom? That's my desk, right?" The other shapes were the front wall and a couple of whiteboards.

Noah didn't answer, biting his lip in concentration as he extended the drawing. He had no grasp of perspective. He kept trying to draw the ceiling as a perfect square, so that it distorted the walls.

"That's not quite it," David said. He pointed at the line where the ceiling met the side wall. "Look again. You're drawing what you *think* you see. What do you *actually* see?"

Noah erased the last few lines, drummed his pencil against the desk, and tried again. But he re-drew the same square ceiling.

"Um, no. I know it's tough. Here, put your hand up. Like you're drawing the edge of the ceiling. See which way your hand goes." He demonstrated, moving an imaginary pencil through the air above his head.

Noah stared at the paper, lower lip thrust out.

"This won't work if you don't look at the thing you're trying to draw." He heard the frustration in his own voice and tried to suppress it. "Here." David picked up the eraser and rubbed out the nearest ceiling line. "You need to—"

Noah re-drew the line. He drew it in the same place as before.

The eraser bent as David's fingers clenched. "Doing the same thing over and over doesn't work when you're doing it wrong."

Noah put the tip of the pencil against the paper, pressing harder and harder. The lead broke, and he dragged the jagged end up the page, gouging the paper, darkening the line he'd already drawn.

David said, "No!"

Noah shrieked, "Fuck you!" and broke the pencil in half. And suddenly David was standing, his hands full of Noah's shirt, yanking him out of his chair and hoisting him into the air. The boy's eyes, wide and terrified six inches from his own, jolted David out of his fury. He set Noah down carefully and walked out into the hall.

He pressed the heels of his hands against his eyes and breathed in deeply through his nose.

When he put his hands down Ms. Cleary stood in front of him. "Go," she said. "Get out of here. And don't come back."

David entered the Plaid Platypus like a bit player in Beau Geste staggering at last into a desert oasis. He put one butt cheek onto a stool, stretched out his bad leg, leaned an elbow on the bar, and sighed in relief.

Moe sauntered over, pulling out his phone to check the time. He raised a quizzical eyebrow.

"Rye and ginger. Please."

Moe's left eyebrow rose to join the right one. David invariably drank beer when he had money, Coke when he was broke. Moe didn't speak, just mixed the drink and slid it across the bar.

David drained half the tumbler, then stared into the drink as a line of warmth formed from his throat to his stomach and spread outward. He considered his options, listened carefully to an inner voice that told him to save his money, then shrugged inwardly and finished the whiskey. He pushed the tumbler toward Moe. "Hit me again."

A fresh tumbler appeared. Moe, however, didn't quite let go of it. "You want to tell me about it?"

David did his best to take the drink. The tumbler didn't move. He heaved an aggrieved sigh. "Bitch cut me loose."

"Ouch." Moe's face crinkled in sympathy, and he let go of the tumbler. "That's rough."

"It was overdue," said David sourly. "Should've told her off months ago."

"I thought ...."

"I mean, how much petty humiliation is one man supposed to take?" He took a deep drink. "Fuck her."

"Word," said Moe, and held out a fist. They bumped knuckles, and David drank again.

"Don't worry about it." Moe reached across the bar and clapped him on the shoulder. "You can do better."

"Sure," said David, as the glow from the whiskey abruptly faded. "I mean, look how great my life was before." *It's back to minimum wage. Longer hours, less pay, and zero job satisfaction.*

"The city's full of women. We'll find you one that isn't so stuck up."

For several long moments David tried to parse this statement, wondering if the whiskey was hitting him faster than he realized. The second tumbler was, somehow, empty. *Am I drunk? No, it's not me.* He looked at his friend. "What the hell are you talking about?"

"Ashley." Moe took the tumbler and replaced it with a tall glass of water. "You can do better than her."

"What? No I can't!" David tried a sip of water and pushed the glass away. "That's crazy talk." He gestured at the empty tumbler. "Gimme another one of those, those, whatever that was."

Moe pushed the water glass closer. "Sure. Listen. Did Ashley break up with you, or not?"

"No!" David backtracked through the conversation and started to laugh. In his peripheral vision he saw heads turning toward him. *I'm laughing too loud.* He wasn't sure if it was alcohol or frayed nerves, and he decided he didn't care.

"I got fired."

Moe made a patting gesture with his hands. "Use your inside voice."

"Sorry."

"Don't worry about it. There's lots of jobs."

Sure, Moe. For guys like you there's always lots of work. For guys like me there's convenience stores and gas stations.

"I'll ask around. We'll find you something in no time. You'll see." He gave David an encouraging smile.

You believe it, too, don't you? High school's over and you're still the cool jock. Everybody likes you. Everybody wants to hire you. And you think it'll be the same for me. You really have no clue. He thought about trying to explain the enormous gulf between their lives, but Moe would never understand.

"Give me another drink," was all he said.

Moe's features tightened as he turned away. By the time he returned with a full tumbler his smile was back. "You had me going for a minute there. I thought Ashley was single. I was gonna catch her on the rebound."

David wrapped a hand around the tumbler because it gave him something to squeeze and made it easier to hide a rising fury. *He's your friend,* said a calm voice in his head. *He's making a joke. He's not going to steal your girlfriend.*

He's always had it so easy, said another voice. *He gets what he wants, and he wants Ashley.*

"Hey, whoah, buddy, slow down."

David looked from Moe to the tumbler, which was inexplicably empty. "I guess I need a refill."

"Not today you don't."

Resentment flared, bright and hot. David thought about banging his tumbler on the bar and demanding another drink. Instead he said, "Stay away from Ashley."

Moe laughed, then tried to hide his amusement. "Sure, Dave. No problem."

"You don't even like her."

Moe held his hands up, palms out. "I—"

"No, that's not it. You DO like her. But she never liked you. She thought you were dumb." David nodded. The rapid head movement made the room spin in a fun way, so he did it again. "Big, strong Moe Pezhman, and Ashley Thomson wouldn't give him the time of day."

Moe's face went blank. "She wasn't my type."

"Of course she was! I saw how you looked at her. You wanted her! Admit it."

Moe glanced around and made a calming gesture with his hands.

I'm too loud. Well, so what? "She thought you were a meathead. You must have hated that." David scanned the area behind the bar. "Moe? Where'd you go?" A heavy hand landed on his shoulder. "Oh! There you are."

Moe levered him off the stool. "Time to go, David."

Pain lanced through David's knee, and he clutched Moe's arm for support. "Come with me. We'll go see Ashley."

"I have to work." Moe hauled David gently but inexorably toward the door.

David clung to his arm, trying to keep weight off his bad leg. "When do you get off?"

"Seven."

"I'll come back."

"You'll still be sleeping it off."

David took a wrong step, and his bad leg buckled. Moe, grumbling, hauled him up and dumped him in a chair. "You can stay if you keep quiet and drink water."

David sat, watching the room spin, an ugly stew of emotions churning in his guts. He felt belligerent and frustrated. He was ashamed of getting fired, ashamed of how long he'd put up with Cleary and her petty humiliations. He was ashamed of the spectacle he was making of himself, and the shame fuelled his anger. He knew it was irrational. He wasn't sure he cared.

"Call me tomorrow," Moe said gently. "We'll find you a new gig. There's lots of ways to make a living."

"What do you know about it?" Moe's hurt, annoyed look just fanned the flames. "Ashley was right about you. You're a meathead. I don't need your help. I don't want to end up in a brain-dead bartending job like you."

Moe's face twitched. "Oh, the mighty goddess Ashley, the woman who's so discerning, she's wasting her life with a drunk loser who can't even hold a job. You know what? Maybe I *should* walk you over to her place. Let her take a really good look at you. See who she chooses this time."

David surged to his feet.

Moe sneered at him. "Go home, David. Don't come back until you're ready to apologize."

David hit him. Or at least, that's what he tried to do. Moe leaned back, David's fist whizzed past his nose, and strong fingers closed on David's wrist.

"Leggo of me."

Moe responded by twisting his arm. David yelped, the pressure bending him forward. The next thing he knew he was stumbling out the front door to land on his hands and knees on the sidewalk in front.

His bad knee thumped into concrete, and for a time he just knelt there, head hanging, lost in a world of bright pain. Shoes moved at the fringes of his vision as people stepped around him.

By the time he made it to his feet he felt coldly sober. He leaned on the front wall of the bar, breathing in short gasps, waiting for the worst of the pain to subside. At last he straightened up. *Okay, David. You've had your little tantrum. You've wallowed in self-pity. Now it's time to pull yourself together.*

He would come back to the Platypus tomorrow. He would apologize. Then he'd go job-hunting. He desperately wanted to see Ashley, but first things first. There was one more thing he could do to clean up the mess he'd made.

Nineteen

David phoned his sister. Emily was distracted and impatient, but she gave him Grandpa's phone number and address. David dialled with only mild anxiety. It was time to act on decisions he had made long ago. It was time to make amends. Time to take responsibility for his life.

There was no answer.

The cab dropped him off in front of a small, neat house in an older suburb. There was no answer when he rang the bell. He tried the handle.

The door was unlocked.

He walked in. "Grandpa?"

The house was well-kept, but showed the strain of the last several days; there were dirty glasses on the coffee table, a shirt draped over the back of a chair. The air felt thick and stuffy and much too warm.

The lights were off, the curtains drawn. The open door splashed a rectangle of light across the carpet. Something moved in the shadows, a bony arm rising to block the light. It was Grandpa, slumped in an easy chair in the corner.

David's spirits immediately rose. "Uh, hi, Grandpa. Um, are you okay?"

Grandpa stood, wobbled, and shifted so he was straddle-legged. He swayed as he peered at his grandson, then exhaled noisily. A wave of stale bourbon breath washed over David.

"So, you little bastard, you finally came to see me?" There was belligerence and mockery in his voice. A familiar grin crossed the grizzled features. It was Dad's grin, the one he wore in his nastiest moods.

Blood rushed into David's head. Somewhere in the back of his mind a calm voice reminded him that the man had just lost his wife. He was upset. And drunk. David shouldn't mind anything he said.

The rest of David reeled.

Grandpa sensed it and pressed his attack. "Well, David, you stupid little turd. You finally got your shit together and came to see me. Well, here I am! Hey, want a drink?" He stooped, fumbled around, and came up with a bottle. He waved the bottle around by the neck as he continued.

"Came to visit your ol' Grandpa. What a good little fucker you are. You were always my favourite. You always do what you're told."

A spurt of liquid shot out the neck of the bottle and splashed over his hand. He peered myopically at the wet spot.

David's field of vision constricted, everything turning grey and blurring around the edges. He struggled to breathe. *He doesn't mean it. It's okay. He's just trying to*

hurt you because he's hurt. It doesn't mean anything.
Hey, at least you know why Dad hates him so much.

Grandpa lurched toward him. "I fought my own son for you, David. I'm alone in my old age because of you. I drove my child away for you. And now you come strolling in here with that stupid smile like you're doing me some kind of favour."

They stood nose to nose, the whiskey breath rolling across David's face. The old man's voice became low and menacing, a harsh grate like metal grinding on stone.

"I don't need any favours from a fuckup like you. The day I lean on a half-baked asswipe like you is the day I join Marilyn in a cemetery. Do you understand that, Shit-For-Brains?"

The room tilted, and David had to stick a foot out to one side to keep his balance. He could see a little area from the bridge of Grandpa's nose to the tip of his chin. Everything else was a smoky blur. He stared, numb and silent, unable to move, waiting for the next blow.

Grandpa's voice was like a gunshot, making David jump. "Do you?"

And then he swung the bottle.

It banged off David's head, without much force. David yelped and spun, running blindly into the door frame with enough force to knock himself down. Grandpa threw the bottle while he was getting up. It thumped solidly into David's spine, stopping him for an instant with a spasm of pain. Then he was up, clawing at the wall. Eventually his grasping fingers found the open doorway and he ran out.

David sat hugging himself on the bus, eyes closed. Things were bad, there was no question of that. His life was unravelling, but he supposed he would survive. He still had one anchor, one touchstone that was better than all the things he had lost put together. As long as he still had Ashley he would be all right. He sniffled, wiped his cheeks, and managed a small smile. It would be good to see her.

He didn't know it was already too late.

Twenty

David strode from one end of the park to the other, waiting for the shards of memory to lose their fresh, sharp edges. *I'm going to have to tell Grandpa I'm innocent. He probably thinks he drove me over the edge.* He still held the phone in his hand. He tapped it awake and read the message.

> *Dear David,*
>
> *I kept this for years. I finally got it scanned. I thought you should have a copy, since if your father ever finds the print he'll probably throw it out.*
>
> *I hope you're doing well at school. I hope you visit us soon.*
>
> *Love,*
> *Mom*

There was one attachment, a photo. It showed a little boy standing in front of a duck pen, fingers hooked through the wire, spellbound. Just behind him was an old man. Unnoticed by the boy, he gazed down at his grandson, his eyes full of love.

David put a fingertip against the screen, feeling older than the man in the picture. "Oh, Grandpa."

Kim watched him from the middle of the park, looking tense and worried. He walked over and took her hand. Her fingers were cold, and he pressed them between his palms. "I'm okay," he said. "But I don't think I have an alibi."

All the determination seemed to have drained out of her. She said, "What do we do now?"

"I'm going back to Moe's place. I'll wait until he wakes up, and I'll talk to him. I need to get ahold of my grandfather, too. Maybe I can phone him. I might not be able to, after I'm arrested." He let go of her hand, but she held on to him. "You, though, need to go home."

She shook her head.

"Look. I can't tell you how much it means to me, the way you've helped me today." He looked down at their intertwined fingers. "I really can't. There aren't any words that are big enough. It's going to sustain me through whatever comes next. But we're getting into the final reel." He saw confusion on her face and sighed. "No one watches the classics anymore."

"I'm going with you."

"You wanted to help me. You've done that. Now it's time to focus on you not getting arrested for aiding a fugitive or something. Or getting shot by some nervous cop. Seriously." He gave her fingers a squeeze. "Go home."

She murmured something too soft for him to hear.

"Sorry?"

"I said, make me." Just like that, the old Kim was back. "Let's not argue." She let go of his hand. "I'll be at Moe's."

She walked away, and all he could do was follow.

There was a new vehicle in the alley, a pale sedan parked near the van. The headlights came on as they emerged from the pathway. "Probably nothing," said David, but they picked up their pace, almost running to Moe's yard. David locked the back door.

Kim went to the kitchen, where she looked out the back window. "Uh-oh."

He didn't have to ask. He could see red and blue lights playing across her face.

David peeked through the front curtains. Nothing moved in the street, and he frowned, perplexed. He pulled one curtain back and looked down the street, in time to see the first police cruiser arrive. It stopped a couple of houses down, lights flashing. He looked the other way. An unmarked car at the curb two doors down suddenly lit up, flashers in the grill strobing as the driver's door opened and a uniformed cop climbed out.

"Well, hell." He let the curtain fall back into place, feeling strangely relieved. At least he could stop waiting for the hammer to fall. "I guess we're done."

Kim pressed herself against his back, wrapping her arms around his waist. "No. Not yet."

"Kim-"

"No. They can't have you yet." She tightened her arms, and he wheezed. "I won't let them."

"Kim." He tried to pry her arms loose, then gave up and rested his hands on hers. "Oh, Kim."

When she finally let go of him it was to check her vibrating phone. "Dad," she said, glancing at the screen. A tap stopped the vibrating. "I really can't handle him right now."

She was sliding the phone into her pocket when it buzzed again. She tapped, brought the phone to her ear, and said, "What?" Her eyes got bigger. "Yes. Um, yes. No." She looked at David, pointed at the phone, and pointed outside. When he gave her a baffled look she rolled her eyes.

"Okay, listen," she said. "It's only a small gun. I don't think he really wants to use it. Give me some time and I think I can talk him down."

"Kim!"

She shushed him. "No, it's okay. I better talk to him, though. Get him calmed down." Her lips curled up in a mischievous smirk, but her voice was cold and weary as she said, "Look, I'll call you back, okay? I can get him to give himself up. No, I'll call you back." She broke the connection and grinned at him.

"Jesus Christ, Kim, this isn't a game!"

She waved a dismissive hand. "It worked, didn't it?"

"Now they think I have a gun!"

"Not really." She nodded toward the street. "He didn't believe me." David sputtered, and she said, "They'll take things slow. Just in case. I bet it'll be hours before they do anything rash."

"Do anything rash, like shoot me? Maybe shoot you too, by accident?" He flapped his arms, feeling ridiculous but unable to restrain himself. "What are you doing?"

"I'm buying us time," she said coolly.

"Time for what?"

"For Moe to wake up. He's our last chance."

"I told you, I left the Platypus at, like, five."

"You don't remember everything, do you? Well, maybe you went back at seven to apologize." She shrugged. "Failing that, maybe you can get Moe to lie."

David, with no idea how to answer that, lapsed into silence. *I need to walk out the front door and surrender. It's not like she can stop me.* He gave Kim a wary glance. *She might just tackle me. Hold me in a headlock until Moe wakes up.*

Kim gazed back at him, her face as placid as if she was in police standoffs every day. Then her forehead crinkled. "I think the stress is finally getting to me."

"Why?"

"I hear elephants."

He stared at her, started to speak, then hesitated. There was a sound, just at the edge of hearing. The distant, angry trumpeting of a bull elephant.

"What the hell?" He looked at the front window. "The cops are using elephants now?"

"Maybe it's a new siren," she said. "It stopped now."

He listened. Instead of an elephant he heard the murmur of a man's voice. The murmuring grew in volume, and footsteps creaked on the basement stairs.

"Dorkiest ringtone ever," Kim said.

Moe shuffled into the kitchen and stopped, bleary eyes looking from David to Kim and back again. He shook his head wearily, then held out a cell phone to David. "It's for you."

David took the phone. "Moe …."

Moe lifted a hand, palm out. He turned without speaking and walked out of the kitchen, lumbering down the hallway to the bathroom.

David lifted the phone to his ear. "Hello?"

"Is this David Parkinson?" It was a man's voice, deep and calm.

"Yes."

"There's rather a lot of police officers gathered outside the house right now, David. We're concerned about Mohammed and Kim. Do we need to be concerned?"

"Um, not overly, no."

"That's good. Are you armed, David?"

He weighed his options. "Maybe."

"It would be best if you gave yourself up. The longer this goes on, the greater the chance that someone will get hurt."

"Sure."

"Would you come outside? Alone and with your hands empty? Just so there's no misunderstandings."

A toilet flushed, and a tap turned on. "In a minute."

"It would be best if—"

"In a minute, I said!" He glared at the phone. *Better calm down. You don't want the cops getting worried.* "Look," he added in a gentler tone. "I need to talk to Moe. Once we've had a chat I'll surrender."

"If I could—"

David hung up on him.

Kim, phone in hand, gave him a glum look and said, "Yay. We're on the news again. It's just like old times." She showed him the screen.

A woman with gleaming teeth held a microphone and gazed into the camera. Behind her a small crowd pressed close to lines of police tape in front of Moe's house. The woman's lips moved, but David was only able to catch a few words. "Hostage." "Murder." His own name.

"Looks like my arrest will be on camera." He gave her a gallows grin. "How's my hair?"

"Painfully unhip. I've been meaning to say something."

He snorted, then looked at the corridor leading to the bathroom. "What's he *doing* in there?"

"You really want to know? I don't."

They waited, watching the news with morbid curiosity. The street scene vanished, replaced by a man who gave a background summary of the deaths of Ashley and Cameron.

When a worn-looking woman with graying hair appeared, Kim turned up the volume.

"It was horrible." She leaned toward the camera, face solemn and eyes big as she spoke. "That poor woman. I have kids of my own, you know? She got the news right here at work. She was on the noon to midnight shift. The call came right before she would of left."

David leaned closer.

"It was so awful, you can't imagine. You can't comfort a person at a time like that. The poor, poor woman. She lost her son."

The shot changed to a view of Moe's house, glowing red and blue in the police lights. David and Kim exchanged glances. "Holy shit," she said. "She has to be talking about Sunrise Macallister."

He nodded. "So much for his alibi."

Nathan's mother had lied.

After a time the sink stopped running, but it was several more minutes before Moe appeared. He dropped into a seat at the end of the kitchen table. "Table's clean," he said. "Now I know I'm dreaming."

"This is Moe," David said. "Moe, this is Kim. She's Ashley's sister."

"Well, I guess that explains why you're breathing." Moe grimaced. "Sorry. That might not have been the most sensitive thing to say. I'm just, you know, not entirely convinced this is real."

"Whatever," she said impatiently. "When was the last time you saw David?"

"Um, like, ten minutes ago? I gave him my phone."

"Before that," she said, exasperated. "Before today."

Moe's face sagged into gloomy folds. "The day he got arrested. When Ashley died. He came to the pub and I threw him out." He gave David a haunted look. "I'm sorry, man."

Before David could answer, Kim interrupted. "You didn't see him again that day? Are you sure?"

"I'm sure, all right." Moe looked down at his hands. "If only ...."

"Let it go," David said gently. "You didn't do anything wrong."

Moe whispered, "Yes I did."

"Bullshit. Listen. You did nothing wrong. Actually, neither did I."

Moe looked up, puzzled.

"I didn't do it, Moe." David rubbed his forehead. "I don't remember everything. But I'm pretty sure it was a guy named Nathan Bagwell. Either him, or his brother Cameron, or both of them together." He shrugged. "It's a long story. But the point is, it wasn't me. So, if you're beating yourself up because you think you drove me to murder, you can stop."

The three of them went silent. After a time David said, "I need to call my grandfather. If he sees this on TV he'll be freaking out." He caught the expression on Moe's face. "What?"

Moe gave him a hunted look. "I'm sorry, man."

"What?" David's throat closed up. He had to force the words out. "What is it?"

"It was on Calgary Tonight," Moe said miserably. "They did a piece on the aftermath of the tragedy. They wanted to interview me, but I told them to fuck off."

David didn't speak, just stared at him.

211

"I'm sorry. He ... your grandfather passed away."

"What ...." David's voice was a hoarse whisper. He cleared his throat. "What happened?"

Moe shook his head.

"Damn it, what happened?"

"He ... he committed suicide. Like, two weeks after the murders."

It hurt less than David would have expected. After so many blows he was too numb to feel much from one more impact. He stared at his hands, noting absently that Kim was squeezing his fingers. Silence filled the kitchen.

After a time Moe spoke. "That cop on the phone said I should sneak out the back. I didn't believe him. I didn't believe you were really here." He shook his head. "It's good to see you, buddy. I didn't think I'd ever see you again."

"It's good to see you too." David smiled. Moe smiled back. They solemnly exchanged knuckle bumps while Kim shook her head.

"Okay," said David when this ritual was complete. "Surrender time. Should I go first?"

"I'll go," said Moe. "I'll tell them you're not dangerous." He heaved himself to his feet. "How do I look?"

David looked him up and down. "Sketchy as hell."

"Good. That's what I was going for." He walked to the front door, opened it a crack, stuck an arm out, and waved. When no gunfire erupted, he stuck out the other hand and waited, giving the cops plenty of time to see he was unarmed. Finally he pushed the door open and walked outside.

Kim and David watched him on the cell phone. A pair of cops rushed up, grabbed his arms, and hustled him away from the house. The camera wobbled and bounced, following Moe's progress until he disappeared behind a police van. Then the camera swung back to the front door of the house.

"Well," Kim said. "I guess I shouldn't keep my public waiting." She reached across the table and they clutched each other's hands.

Whatever happens next, I'll have this moment. They have to let me keep it. I don't care if they lock me away, so long as they let me keep my memory.

Except he did care. It wasn't the world outside the Lougheed Institute he wanted to hang onto. It was Kim.

Just Kim.

He pried his fingers loose. "Go. I'll be right behind you."

She stood. "Give me five minutes. So I can tell them you're not dangerous. That there's no gun."

"Five minutes," he said.

She started to speak, then nodded and turned away. She hurried to the front door, as if afraid of losing her nerve. For a moment she was a dark silhouette in the doorway. Then she was gone.

Her phone still lay on the table. He watched nervously as cops hustled Kim away. *She's fine. She's safe. And if there's legal trouble, well, she's the sister of a murder victim. They'll go easy on her.*

The camera returned to the house, the open front door giving it a derelict appearance. *I should shut it behind me on the way out.* David drummed his fingers on the table, waiting for five minutes to pass. *I probably should have checked the time.* He looked at the phone. *If they charge the house I want to see it coming.*

Someone crossed the screen, right behind the reporter. A heavy figure, limping but moving quickly. The figure vanished behind the camera truck before David could get a clear look.

He took the phone to the window and looked out at the lines of tape. The cops had added a couple of sawhorses. There was a commotion at the back of the crowd. Someone jostled a reporter, then waded into the sight-seers, shoving people right and left. A woman behind the nearest sawhorse staggered sideways, and David stiffened.

Nathan Bagwell raised one foot and kicked the sawhorse aside. The closest cop turned, too late, as Bagwell charged past.

The cops had most of their attention focussed inward, on the house. Bagwell caught them by surprise, darting around a squad car. He charged across the lawn, moving fast. Bright squares of bandage showed on his left hand and his temple, covering his self-inflicted cuts. The butcher knife was in his fist. His face was hard and angry.

Two quick strides brought David to the front door. He slammed it shut an instant before Bagwell hit. The door shook, David shot the bolt, and the doorknob rattled furiously.

That was close. David sagged against the door, then looked around for the phone.

A concrete gnome crashed through the picture window, billowed the curtains, and banged into the hardwood floor. Shards of glass rained down. Bagwell appeared a moment later, clambering through the window.

David stood frozen at the front door, staring. Behind Bagwell cops ran across the lawn. Bagwell braced a foot on the bottom of the window frame, his hands stretching past jagged edges of glass, looking for purchase. He let go of the butcher knife to grab the side of the window frame. He heaved himself up and in.

David darted forward and kicked the knife away. Bagwell, bleeding from half a dozen fresh cuts, lunged at him, hands out and grasping. David crashed to the floor with Bagwell on top of him.

Bagwell's hands locked around his throat.

David reached up, prying at the man's wrists. He couldn't breathe. Thick fingers sank into his neck. The room spun.

David thrashed and turned his head, glass cutting into his cheek. Something glinted in the corner of his eye.

It was the knife. He stretched out a hand and felt the prick of glass against his wrist. His fingers curled around hard plastic, and he knew he was going to survive.

He brought the knife up and put the point against the side of Bagwell's neck. He only had a few seconds of consciousness left. He had to do this right.

He stared at the face above him, purplish and ugly with hatred. No one would miss Nathan Bagwell. One quick press, a gush of blood, and David would live.

He dropped the knife.

The room faded. The pain in his neck grew distant. He floated, finding a moment to think regretfully of Kim, who would be devastated. He thought of Moe, who really needed a friend right now. Of Grandpa, who he was too late to help.

Muffled voices yelled. Glass and wood broke. He felt bad for Moe, getting his garbage dump of a house trashed even further, but this wasn't David's doing. He couldn't take responsibility for everything.

The gunshot sounded distant, faint, like someone popping a paper bag. Bagwell jerked, fingers loosening. David's vision cleared in time to see Bagwell cough up a gout of vivid crimson blood. It spattered across David's face.

No, this isn't right. He shouldn't die because of me.

Bagwell shifted and leaned hard on his thumbs. Something broke in David's throat.

Gunfire thundered, merging into a continuous roar. Bagwell jerked sideways as if swatted by a vast hand, and David had time to draw one breath.

Cops stepped forward and flipped David onto his face. They hauled his arms back, and handcuffs clicked into place around his wrists.

Something swelled in his throat. He fought to exhale, managed it, but couldn't inhale. The pressure grew, and with it the pain. *Well, I did my best. At least no one else will get hurt because of me.*

The room went dark. The world faded away and the pain went with it.

Twenty-One

They met in the dog park and followed the edge of the river valley at a slow jog. By the time they reached the first staircase both of them were gasping for breath. Moe led the way down the steps, not even pretending to hurry. David followed.

They alternately walked and jogged beside the river, stopping at the base of the second staircase. Moe gazed upward, his face tragic. "We've made a terrible mistake."

"Maybe we could get an Uber."

"Not the worst suggestion I've heard." Moe sighed theatrically, then started to climb. David plodded up the stairs after him.

At the top they sat on the grass and watched sun and cloud make complex dancing patterns on the water far below. David kneaded his thighs, wondering how long it would take for his muscle tone to return.

"How's the neck?"

David touched his throat, finding a tender spot where the tracheotomy was still healing. "It itches sometimes. But it doesn't hurt to talk."

"Good." Moe looked at him, his expression strangely flat. "What happened with the cops?"

"Well, I was never formally charged, back then." David made a face. "Didn't stop them from handcuffing me to my bed. But by the time I was ready to leave the hospital they said I was free to go. Once I told them everything."

"Everything." Moe's voice, like his face, was unreadable. "What exactly do you mean by 'everything'?"

"I left the Platypus." David flushed. "When you kicked me out. Which I deserved."

Moe nodded without speaking.

"I went to see my grandfather, and he wasn't any more impressed with me than you were. So I went to see Ashley." He looked out across the park, letting emotion rise like a wave and then recede.

"I walked in and saw her body. I thought Cameron Bagwell was dead too. He wasn't moving. I didn't see Nathan until he stabbed me." David touched his stomach. "After that I freaked out pretty bad. I ran outside. I sat in the alley for a while. Then I started walking down the street and screaming. That's when the cops picked me up."

Moe stared at him, not blinking. "Why ...?"

"Why didn't I call 911?"

"Why do you still think you can lie to me?"

David's mouth went dry.

"I understand why you want to. You don't want to tell me you did something bad. Knowing you, you're probably scared I'll get back on fentanyl." Moe looked down, shredding blades of grass with his thumbnail. "I was in this pattern after you got locked up. I kept seeing your face when I threw you out. Kept imagining you in some awful mental hospital getting electric shock treatment or something. I kept thinking about Ashley. I kept thinking it was my fault."

He brushed bits of grass from his shoe and looked at David. "But it wasn't my fault. You broke the pattern when you came back. You woke me up a bit. Once I stopped ...." He made a face. "Well, I'm all done being a fat slob. I'm not going back. So don't worry about me."

David stared at him helplessly.

"Tell me the truth." Moe lifted his hands, palms up. "Who else can you tell?"

"She was the only thing I had left." Once the words started, there was no holding them back. "My whole life was going to shit, but I knew if I still had Ashley, things would be okay. I went to her apartment. I let myself in. I heard a sound from the bedroom. She was with Cameron. They were naked. She had her legs wrapped around his waist, and she looked ... ecstatic. I just went nuts. I never decided to, to do what I did. It just happened." A sob tried to choke him, but he forced it down. "God forgive me, I killed both of them. I stabbed them to death with a pair of scissors. And when it was over, I tried to kill myself. I stabbed myself in the stomach. But I didn't die. And now it looks like I'll get away with it."

He squeezed his eyes shut and heard again the last gurgle she'd made before she went silent. He would spend the rest of his life trying to make up for that sound.

"I can't tell the cops." He glanced at Moe, then looked away. "Kim and Aaron ... they were just about destroyed by the murder. Now they think something good finally came from it all. Justice prevailed. They helped free an innocent man. I'm like a symbol of hope for them. If I confess now ...."

A bit late to think about consequences, said a cold voice in his head. Still, late or not, his actions did have consequences. If his silence could repair a tiny bit of the damage he'd done, then he would keep his lips sealed.

Moe said gently, "Nathan Bagwell had family too."

"I know. But Nathan is dead. He died trying to murder me. Or execute me, if that's the way you see it. The most I can offer his family is, what? A chance to believe he was only moderately homicidal."

A pregnant silence stretched out. Moe sighed, then climbed slowly to his feet. "Things have a way of eating at a man. Believe me, I know. You have to find a way to be at peace with yourself. To forgive yourself. Otherwise it was all for nothing." He shook his legs out one at a time. "Looks like your ride is here."

A familiar blue Civic rolled to a stop on the far side of the park. Sunlight glittered on the windshield, turning Aaron into a vague blur behind the wheel. Kim climbed out of the passenger seat and waved.

Moe reached a hand down and helped David to his feet. "Same time next week?"

David nodded, got a slap on the back in reply, and turned toward the car. Kim smiled and held out her hand, and he came forward to meet her.

Mentions

Dwayne Clayden helped keep the cop-related stuff realistic. Juan Valdez was essential to the writing and editing process (the book is more coffee than ink, at this point). My wife Tammy was supportive and patient and generally cheered me on as I grappled with the muse. The book is much, much better because I got to work with an uncommonly good editor, Sarah L. Johnson. The parts you don't like are my fault. Don't blame these guys.

About the Author

Brent Nichols is a Calgary-based novelist, bon vivant, and man about town, with hobbies that include kickboxing, digital painting, and pun fests. He writes science fiction under the pen name Jake Elwood, but when his steely eye and battered keyboard turn to the mean streets of Gotham North (By the way, we're calling Calgary "Gotham North" now. Tell your friends.) he writes without the protection of a pseudonym. This is his first book with Tiny Sledgehammer.

Visit us online at
www.the-seventh-terrace.com/tiny-
sledgehammer